AMBROSIA LEE DROPS THE MIC

ALSO BY PATRICIA PARK

Imposter Syndrome and Other Confessions of Alejandra Kim

What's Eating Jackie Oh?

AMBROSIA LEE DROPS THE MIC

PATRICIA PARK

CROWN
New York

Crown Books for Young Readers
An imprint of Random House Children's Books
A division of Penguin Random House LLC
1745 Broadway, New York, NY 10019
penguinrandomhouse.com
rhcbooks.com

Library of Congress Cataloging-in-Publication Data is available upon request.

ISBN 979-8-217-02976-1 (trade)—ISBN 979-8-217-02978-5 (ebook)

The text of this book is set in 11.5-point Bembo MT Pro.

Manufactured in the United States of America
1st Printing

The authorized representative in the EU for product safety and compliance is Penguin Random House Ireland, Morrison Chambers, 32 Nassau Street, Dublin D02 YH68, Ireland, https://eu-contact.penguin.ie.

Random House Children's Books supports the First Amendment and celebrates the right to read.

This novel is dedicated to Brett Taylor, for enduring this stand-up research journey with me.

ACT I

DRAMA

All the world's a stage,
And all the men and women merely players . . .

—William Shakespeare, *As You Like It*

1

TRAGIC BACKSTORY

Every character needs a tragic backstory, so here's mine: I was a child actor who peaked at twelve, and now I'm a sixteen-year-old has-been. Not that playing a dead body on *Law & Order* counts as *having been* anything.

I was "discovered" on the subway when I was seven years old. Back then, no lie, I was *adorable*: peaches-and-cream face with rosy-red cheeks, big dark eyes with double-creased lids, and shiny black hair that, on that fateful day, Mom decided to braid into pigtails. I looked like a porcelain china doll. A perky Wednesday Addams. There totally would've been a hit on me if literal headhunting was still a thing.

Ever since I was a kid, people would stop Mom and Dad on the street: "What a *beautiful* child!" They'd pick apart my features—"Ooh, her father's eyes, her mother's hair!"—like they were triumphantly solving the jigsaw puzzle that was me. Sometimes I liked it; mostly I hated it.

At banquets, our relatives would say in disbelief to Mom,

"How could such a pretty child come from someone as plain as you?" Mom would just laugh it off—those were the days she was actually happy—but it always made me mad. Not that I was allowed to speak out to my elders. Dad, who doesn't know Korean beyond *kimchi* and *galbi*, would just smile and nod politely.

Ever since their divorce, Dad doesn't come to family functions on Mom's side anymore. I think he thinks they'll blame him. But what he doesn't know is, almost two years later, the relatives are still on Mom's case about *her* being the one who chased Dad away.

"AMBROSIA LEE" IS—WAS—MY STAGE name. You'd think Ambrosia is the made-up part, but that is 100 percent what's printed on my birth certificate. My legal last name is Blacksmith. Yeah, yeah, I get it: *food of the gods!* doesn't exactly jibe with hammers and anvils and all. We went with Mom's maiden name, Lee, which has a way nicer ring. Plus it protects my privacy from creepos.

Once upon a time, it was fun to play make-believe. I was Brosh at home, Ambrosia Lee in the business, but onstage I could pretend to be *anybody*. I'd fall into character and imagine her yesterday, today, and tomorrow.

I loved—still love—being in the spotlight. (TBH, I'm kind of a ham.) But lately, the few scripts that come my way are so one-dimensional, which just kind of makes you feel dead inside. That's if I'm lucky enough to land the work at all. The roles have dried up. I haven't booked a gig in over a year. That's a lifetime in child acting—which is like Narnia, but with none of the perks of talking fauns or Turkish delight. (Plenty of white witches, though.)

I'm in that nebulous age range of fourteen to seventeen, where child actors go to die. Post-puberty, we're too old to play kids but too young to play our actual age. Most of us don't survive adolescence. For every Selena Gomez who gracefully transitioned from child star to adult A-lister, there's a blowup and burnout like Amanda Bynes. And for every one of *them*, there were millions of girls who shot their shot but fell into obscurity. Any one of them would have killed for their five seconds of fame.

And don't even get me started on Britney.

Ever since I was a kid, acting has been the only path I've known. I doubt I'll get into a good college because I was never focused on my grades; all my "free" time was devoted to going to auditions and memorizing scripts. I don't know if I should return to Gotham Drama School or transfer to a "regular," non–performing arts high school, where I won't be surrounded by A-listers in training. I also got into LaGuardia—the free, public version of GDS—but that'll just be more of the same. I don't need the daily FOMO about the roles my classmates got that I was rejected for.

I've all but given up on my "dream" to act on Stage and Screen. Some days, I wonder if it was ever my dream in the first place.

Now that my "career" is in air quotes, I have no idea what to do with the rest of my life.

2

STAN THE MAN (OR SO HE LIKES TO TELL HIMSELF)

Stan, my on-again, off-again talent agent, calls about an audition for E-Z Klean Bleach, *now in spray-bottle form!*

"I had to pull some serious strings, Broshie!" Stan says it in his usual overselling-it way, which is practically a prerequisite for being an agent.

He has two modes: gushing or ghosting.

"The same cattle call I saw posted on Backstage?" I ask.

"Very funny. If this commercial gets picked up for national syndication, you'll be laughing all the way to the bank, trust me."

"Stan, do you look at me and only see dollar signs?"

Mom, who's also on the call, shoots me a *be nice* look.

"With all due respect, Broshie," Stan says, "you haven't earned me a penny in over a year."

"Not true," I say. "I just got my residuals from *Law & Order*."

It was for twenty-three cents. The stamp cost more than the check itself.

"Broshie, Broshie, Broshie," Stan says. "E-Z Klean's the first real nibble we've had in ages."

Mom jumps in. "Stan, of course we understand. Things have changed. Brosh is a . . . harder sell than she once was."

Mom glances at me apologetically as she says it. But at this point, I've grown numb to hearing myself talked about in dollars and cents.

Dead Asian Girl #3 on *Law & Order* was not actually the biggest role I had.

It was Golly Jee on *Jump! Rope! Jungle!*

The show was a zany mix of sketch comedy, balloon blizzards, and slime. It made Nielsen's top ten most-viewed children's shows of all time. *Jump! Rope! Jungle!* was supposed to be my big break.

But I got fired from season 1.

"Not gonna lie, we're in no-man's-land, Cindy," Stan says to Mom. "But there are things Brosh could do to make herself more sellable, like she did in the past. We had some near chances two pilot seasons ago, if only Brosh—"

"What about *Leviathan*?" I interrupt.

Leviathan, an Emmy-winning ABC ensemble dramedy set in a cutthroat white-shoe law firm, is the best thing on prestige TV right now. It's equal parts *Succession*, *Modern Family*, and—twist—*How to Get Away with Murder*. The part I read for was Katie Chung: the snarky teen daughter of one of the series regulars, Claudia Chung (Asian female, 30s, type-A Ivy Leaguer clawing for partner). I only had a day to prepare my self-tape, so I skipped class to memorize my sides (industry-speak for the script for your part), Mom helping me run lines. I did take after take until it was perfect.

Katie Chung is a dream role—even if it's only a guest spot.

Mom and I hunker down to watch *Leviathan* every other Sunday night, when I'm not at Dad's. The show's pretty much the only thing holding us together at this point.

"Still no news. It's ABC, Broshie. I wouldn't get my hopes up," Stan says. "I know it feels like taking a step backward with these commercials. But this is just a stepping stone to the NEXT BIG THING!"

Stan is the only person I know who speaks in all caps, like a bad script.

I do that stagey thing where I air-pinch my face and close my eyes. "I am a vessel, I am a vessel . . ."

It's an old cliché: Actors are just "vessels" for other people's stories.

"Save the drama for the screen," Stan says, but I can hear him struggling not to laugh.

Mom puts the call on mute. "Brosh, I wish you'd show some gratitude. You heard Stan. This commercial could go national."

I say, "Great. I'll be the next Flo from Progressive Insurance!"

"Hate all you want," Mom says. "That woman's set for life."

I know Mom and Stan are right. Commercials, if you're lucky enough to land one, can be great gigs. Even if there's only so much acting you can do in a thirty-second time slot.

Every day, I scroll through the listings on Backstage, and it's the same depressing stereotypes: martial artists, "model minorities," or "illegal" immigrants. Sometimes it's a three-fer, and you're expected to play a karate-chopping straight-A student with a perfect SAT score and a tragic undocumented backstory. At best a supporting role—but never the lead.

They must think we lack Main Character Energy.

"We just can't afford to blow another big break."

Mom's words cut me. I know I'm a disappointment. *You're not special just because you're on TV*, as my older brother, Ryan, used to say to me. He's right. My parents have poured so much into my career—time, energy, and money they'll never get back. Mom, who went to Parsons, quit her job as a fashion designer for a Garment District wholesaler to become a full-time stage mom. Now she's divorced and underemployed. Her only income is some freelance tailoring jobs and the rent that comes in from our downstairs tenants in our two-family in Maspeth, which mostly goes back into fixing up the house. That's it.

Mom unmutes the call. "Thank you so much, Stan! We're so grateful for all you do for Brosh."

She says it in her try-too-hard voice, the same one she uses with all industry people.

Even the ones who fired me.

3

E-Z KLEAN

So I go to the E-Z Klean audition. I'm in a waiting room full of my doppelgängers. We're all competing for the privilege of reciting this gem of a script:

MOM (Unidentified Asian Female, ages 30–39) and DAUGHTER (UAF, ages 12–18) are on their hands and knees, scrubbing a filthy bathroom. Mom sprays a black spot with E-Z Klean Bleach.

DAUGHTER

Look, Ma! It's getting whiter!

CUT TO: Mom and Daughter wearing all white in a sparkling white bathroom.

MOM

Make your life whiter—and brighter!
That's why my family chooses
E-Z Klean Bleach—

DAUGHTER

Now in spray-bottle form!

Mom is sitting next to me. I'm sixteen, yet she still insists on accompanying me to my auditions because I'm technically a minor. All morning, she's been on my case about doing "character work" for my UAF. But there's only so much backstory I can bring to *Now in spray-bottle form!*

Mom's flipping through the celebrity tabloids. "Has Gwynnie put on weight?" she asks, nudging me.

"Mom, the woman drinks bone broth on a *cheat* day."

She turns the page. "Oh! It was just the ski suit. *Very* unflattering."

"I'm *trying* to get in the zone," I say. Operative word being *try*. All around me, the other UAFs recite their lines to themselves. The tension is thick. Everybody here wants it *so* badly. I won't lie; it really messes with your head to be in a roomful of people who look exactly like you. Well, *almost* exactly. Am I imagining it when a UAF sizes me up and a smug smile creeps across her face? Nope. Because now another UAF does the same thing—dismissing me with a flick of her eyes.

The only thing all the UAFs have in common is that they are stick thin—and I am not.

I fit into straight sizes, but I'm far from a size two. According to Hollywood, that means I am a cow. That's show business for you: stick or cow. There's no such thing as in between. Which makes me a liability in the biz.

Then I see the UAFs sizing up Mom. I know what they're thinking. It's written all over their faces.

Mom flips the page of her tabloid. "Ooh, she's on The Chip." The Chip is a two-thousand-dollar piece of work-out equipment the size of a potato chip. You know those commercials where it's Christmas morning and the husband surprises—aka body-shames—the wife with The Chip? Yeah, that.

"Maybe we should get The Chip, too." Mom looks down at herself. She's wearing a drab dark poncho thingy that hides her shape. Mom can't shop for clothes in straight-size stores. She used to design her own creations, working her magic on the sewing machine; now she just wears the same old clothes she orders in bulk online.

Then Mom looks me up and down, and I 100 percent infer her meaning.

My phone pings.

Dad:

Hi Brosh, Are you free tomorrow at 9am for breakfast?

Me:

9am??

on a sat???

Dad (angry text forming but his thumbs are too slow):

. . .

Me:

Where

Dad:

Pomegranate

79 Spring St (between Broadway and Crosby)

New York, NY 10012

Me:

Pomegranate's still a thing?

Dad (ignoring my diss):

Please, Ambrosia. It's important.

Mom peers over my shoulder. "Is that your father?"

"Yeah," I say, shielding my screen from her. "We're meeting for breakfast tomorrow." I make my voice sound super casual so I don't set off her suspicions.

Too late. "With *her*?"

Mom's referring to Dad's "lady friend," Nabi.

"I don't know, I guess." I don't feel like getting into it.

"I can't believe your dad's gone native."

"Mom, we're *all* Korean."

Dad was born in Korea but was raised in Minnesota by his Korean mom and his white American stepdad. Mom was born and raised in Maspeth, Queens, to Korean immigrant parents. And Nabi's *Korean* Korean, from Seoul.

"Korean *American*. Big difference," Mom says. "Also, why doesn't your father wait until next week?"

Translation: *Why does he want you during* my *week?* Because this is the reality of living with divorced parents.

I ignore Mom's not-so-rhetorical question and put on my headphones to watch clips of my favorite stand-up comedian, Josie Kang. Comedy helps get me out of my own head when my anxieties are already *up to here*. Josie Kang's from Queens, like me, and speaks truth to power. She'd have a field day with this E-Z Klean script. Josie's performing in New York tomorrow night, but her show completely sold out while the ticket was still in my cart.

As Mom flips through her crappy tabloids and feels worse about herself, as the UAFs murmur their lines, I watch Josie's jokes and forget the world around me.

Try to, anyway.

The door to the casting room opens—and out walks another dejected UAF.

The casting director's assistant looks up from her clipboard. "Ambrosia Lee? You're next."

I SLATE UP FOR the CD, producers, director, and some suits who are probably the E-Z Klean execs.

The CD frowns at my headshot. "You look different since *Jump! Rope! Jungle!*"

"Uh . . . yeah," I say, because what else am I going to say? *It's called puberty*?

The audition is a chem test with Sandy Yang, the actor who'll play my mom. Sandy has a flat, Minnesotan twang, same as Dad's. She's petite, with delicate, birdlike features. She was in that new kung fu movie . . . or was it the geisha show on Netflix? Or was she the dragon lady in the Marvel franchise?

Or maybe it wasn't Sandy Yang at all but some other UAF.

"Mom" and I start the script. We're on our hands and knees, scrubbing the imaginary bathroom. I can already feel it's not a flattering angle because, gravity. As I deliver my lines, the execs "whisper," "Not the right body type."

The CD nods in agreement. "Too chubby."

They're obviously not talking about Sandy Yang. They're talking about me.

I can feel my cheeks burn with humiliation. "Mom" gives me a sympathetic wince, but she doesn't say anything, either.

I wish I were like Josie Kang—no BS, no filter. But I'm just an actor. And actors have to follow the script. I haven't even made it to *Look, Ma!*, when suddenly I find myself veering off script:

"If I got any '*whiter and brighter*,' I'd order a pumpkin-spice latte!"

That gets the table's attention.

I immediately regret the joke. Not just because talking back during an audition is a huge no-no. It's because "PSL Season"—UGG boots and all—is so clichéd. I could've come up with a way funnier line.

"*What* was that?" the CD demands. She nudges her assistant, who is frantically searching her clipboard, like somewhere in those pages is the explanation for my misbehavior.

"Is this some kind of joke to you?" says a producer. "Stick to the script!"

The casting table is now glaring at "Mom," like she's guilty by association. I shoot Sandy an *I'm sorry* look.

"Thank you for your time." I curtsy and get the hell out of there.

I can't believe I just did that. Ambrosia Lee is a rule follower, not a self-sabotager. Stan's going to be so pissed: *I pulled some serious strings to get you that cattle call!*

This audition was my last do-or-die.

Now I've basically lit the bridge behind me.

BACK IN THE WAITING room, my doppelgängers dutifully recite their lines. They all look so hungry for it—figuratively *and* literally.

"How'd it go?" Mom asks. She never comes into the audition room with me because of superstition.

There's so much hope in her eyes. Mom's still clinging to the idea of my Great Comeback. We need this win. I need this, but Mom *really* needs this. Because ever since the divorce, I'm the one who's had to keep it together so Mom wouldn't fall apart. It's like our roles got reversed.

So I tell her what she wants to hear:

"Nailed it."

4

JUMP! ROPE! JUNGLE!

Stan:

You got invited to the Jump! Rope! Jungle! reunion party! It's tonight! My assistant is emailing you the details!

Me:

which one

you go through them like water

Stan:

ha ha

This will be good for you, Broshie! Rub elbows! Network! Drum up some LEADS!!

Me:

thought that was your job

Stan:

I'd come, but we're traveling for my kid's thing. I swear, wife #2 is killing me!!

Me:

you could go back to wife #1

Stan:

Always with the jokes, Broshie!

Me:

any word from the bleach peeps

Stan:

Not yet. WHY? How'd it go?

Me:

nm

Stan:

I already told Nick you'd COME!

Me:

. . .

the guy fired me stan

Stan:

Imagine how bad it'd look if you're a NO-SHOW!!

Me:

100% emotional blackmail

Stan:

100% what makes our industry run

Stan forced me to attend the *Jump! Rope!* reunion party. It's in the gorgeous penthouse of the Hotel East River, and I'm standing awkwardly in the corner, wishing I could disappear.

I spot some of my former castmates, but they either don't see me or pretend they don't. It's bad enough they ignore me in the halls at GDS. They say Hollywood is like high school, but what if your literal high school is *also* Hollywood? Not to sound all dramatic, but I'm kind of a loser at this party.

I text my friend Annie Perkins.

Where are you?

Annie and I came up together in the circuit: classes at the Madame Olga Acting Studio, auditions, callbacks. We were so excited when we both landed roles on *Jump! Rope!* Annie played our ringleader, Perky Freckles, and shot to fame.

I fiddle with my phone, pretending like I'm a Very Important Person, as the painful minutes tick by.

Finally, Annie texts back:

UGHHHH still stuck at this thing

B there soon!!

Nick, the showrunner of *Jump! Rope!*, is working the room like he's the king of the ball. Which he technically is. He spots me and strides over. He's with a random industry type with the same bro-y vibe.

"Ambrosia, bring it in!"

"Hey . . . Nick!" I force a smile and return his hug, because I am a Professional Actor.

"*Super* cool you could drop by!" Nick gets his spray tan on me. It smells terrible, like booze-soaked coconuts. "Stan says you've been keeping *super* busy!"

"Ohmigod, *so* busy!" I say, matching his fake, gushy energy. "It was down to me and Zendaya for *Quantum Echo Hunters*. But she screen-tested better in green."

Random Industry Guy laughs at my joke.

"Yeah, yeah, *totally*!" Nick says, scanning past me for someone more *more*. Big-timing is a favorite pastime in the Entertainment Industrial Complex.

Well, two can play that game. I decide to keep messing with him. "But I *did* beat Selena for the lead in *Transformers: The Musical*." I laugh to sell the bit.

"You're very funny," Random Industry Guy says. "You remind me of a young Josie Kang."

"I love Josie Kang!" I blurt out. "I didn't take you for Kang Gang."

"Why, because I'm a white dude?"

I blush. "Sorry, I mean—"

"Offense taken." But RIG says it good-naturedly. "I'm so Kang Gang, my husband and I are seeing her tomorrow."

Of *course* the Suit nabbed tickets to Josie's sold-out show.

We swap some of our favorite Josie Kang one-liners. Nick joins in the laughter, a beat too late.

"Ambrosia's *hilarious*! *So* missed having you on set! Why did you ever leave us?"

Nick is showbiz bullshit at its finest. He fires me one minute, then laments the fact that I've been fired the next. There's this expression Mom sometimes says: Byeong jugo, yak junda. It means they give you the disease, then they give you the medicine.

Pretty sure it was invented in Hollywood.

Nick cocks a finger gun at me. "Listen, gotta run. *So* great seeing you! Call me!"

It's an empty promise—just like my *Jump! Rope!* contract.

He and Random Industry Guy leave. Nick calls out over his shoulder, "Help yourself to anything here. Eat up!"

The punch line is not lost on me.

Across the room, I spot a girl gliding with belle-of-the-ball energy. She is the life of the party.

It's The Other Jee.

5

THE OTHER JEE

When I was cast as Golly Jee on *Jump! Rope! Jungle!*, I was an eleven-year-old gangly beanpole; by the time we started shooting (strikes, production delays, more strikes), I was thirteen, with T&A incoming. I could not halt the tidal wave that was puberty. Imagine telling an ocean to stop being an ocean.

I got fired after three episodes.

The day I was let go from *Jump! Rope!*, I'd been double-dutching for a scene, when suddenly Nick yelled, "Cut!" For the rest of the episode, they hid me and my "massive" body behind palm trees and bushes. We wrapped, and I was asked to leave the set. Nick made up a storyline to explain my absence: Golly Jee was visiting her sick grandma in Seoul for a few episodes. And when "I" returned to the show—

They replaced me with The Other Jee.

Who was also literally named Jee(sun) Lee.

They didn't even bother to explain the discontinuity on

Jump! Rope! Jungle! It was just—*boop!*—the old switcheroo. No one blinked an eye.

Jeesun Lee and I have a long history. Which is just a nicer way of saying "beef." We'd show up at the same casting calls for *cute Asian girl!* For every role I got, she lost, and vice versa. Until I landed the holy grail.

Until I didn't.

After she replaced me, The Other Jee skyrocketed to fame. She became the second most popular *Jump! Roper!* after Annie, if the McDonald's toy sales are to be believed. She's launching her own perfume line. She's photographed partying with K-pop stars and has millions of followers on social media.

"Ohmigod, Ambrosia Lee? I totally didn't recognize you! What are *you* doing here?" Jee says it in that LA drawl everyone in the industry has down, like a cross between a cheerleader and a stoner.

So I mimic her. "Ohmigod, Jee, it's *been* a minute! How *are* you?"

Jee leans in for a fake kiss. She even *smells* fake, like liquefied Jolly Ranchers. (Her new perfume's called Kandi from Strangers.) Jee is wearing this mini-maxi dress thing, and she's so tiny I could probably strangle her waist with my hands and my fingertips would still touch. Of course I feel hulking by comparison, especially the way she's sizing me up now.

"It's been *forever*!" Jee says, laughing. "I haven't seen you in anything. Did you, like, quit the biz? I *love* that for you!"

I give the line I've been rehearsing in my head: "I'm taking time off to work on the craft as I make the transition to more mature, *challenging* work. Away from all that *kid* stuff."

Jee cocks her head, like she knows I'm just feeding her a line. She takes a sip from her drink. "Who are you *wearing*, Ambrosia?"

I'm wearing a thrift-store find—black blazer and matching dressy shorts with a pink silk cami.

"Costco Couture," I deadpan. "Same aisle as the jumbo pretzel buckets."

It takes a beat for it to land. "You're too funny, Ambrosia," Jee says. "It must be so refreshing to never have to worry about the paps. God, I'm so jealous!"

My cheeks burn from the "compliment." But I can't think of a snapback fast enough.

I should have just stayed home and watched reruns of *Leviathan* with Mom.

"Cut the crap, Jee," says a voice behind us. "You'd kill for Brosh's face and you know it."

It's Annie Perkins. Wearing her Perky Freckles "costume" of a blue gingham petticoat dress, black patent shoes, and white bobby socks. Her strawberry hair is tied in pigtails.

We all air-kiss hello. Annie smells like baby powder, daisies, and cigarettes. "America's sweetheart" smokes half a pack a day and still gets work playing ten-year-olds.

"Ohmigod, Annie!" Jee's putting on her candy-fake voice again. But I can tell she's still smarting from Annie's earlier diss. "I'm *so* sorry to hear you got kicked off that cooking show for, what, a PB and J?"

Annie was a contestant on *Burn Off! Teen Edition*. But she was eliminated in the first round. (Cooking is not her forte.)

"Ohmigod, Jee, you're so sweet!" Annie says. "Can you believe *Burn Off!* wants me back on to guest host? Crazy, right? By the way, I was *so* sorry to hear about what went down with your other 'project.' What was it called again? *Jade Brothel*?" Her voice drips with fake-sympathy.

"*Jade* Hotel," Jee corrects. "Whatever, I *chose* to walk away. Creative differences. Did I just read about your mom in *Star*? I would've been flipping out, but I *love* how you're, like, keeping your cool!"

"God, does anyone still read *Star*?" Annie says. "Bless your heart!"

Jee and Annie volley backhanded compliments like it's the US Open in passive-aggression. It'd be beautiful to watch—if it weren't so ugly.

Jee does an over-the-top glance at her watch. "Much as I *loved* catching up, I've got to run. I have an early morning. Jamie Ha's shopping around a new project, you know."

Annie squints. "Isn't Amy Park up for that?"

But Jee's already sashaying her way through the crowd, leaving us in a cloud of her manufactured candy scent.

"Wow." Annie shakes her head. "She is a piece of work."

"Right?" I say. "Thanks for having my back, Annie."

Annie waves it off like *No biggie*. "The Other Jee is the *worst*. I wish you never left the set, Brosh. Nick and the network fucked you over, big-time. He's such a creep."

"Bygones," I say, because nobody likes a trauma dump.

"You seem to be doing all right for yourself. Last time I saw you, your face was on the side of a bus."

Despite Peanut Buttergate, Annie has now been tapped to host *Kidz Edition*, the children's spin-off of *Burn Off!* She just flew in from LA to film the finale.

Annie groans. "These *Burn Off!* brats can't cook for crap. I didn't even want to do the show, but my team's all, *You need to stay relevant! Reconnect with your core base!* But also at the same time, *Expand your demographic!* Bull. Shit."

"I thought that's what your Hallmark Christmas specials were for?"

"Ha-ha," Annie says. "So what about you? Up for anything?"

"Besides a commercial for E-Z Klean?" I wiggle my spirit fingers.

"My mom's *addicted* to that stuff!" Annie says. "Ugh, wrong word."

"How *is* Donna these days?" I ask.

"No comment," Annie says. "So? Did you get the bleach gig?"

"Nope." As I tell Annie what went down at the audition, I transform it into a funny story, adding comic flourishes. Even though I'm still mortified by my self-sabotage. By the end, Annie is howling with laughter.

"I can't believe you did that," she says, wiping her eyes. "You're either my new shero or a total dumbass."

"Probably both," I admit. "I have no idea what came over me. Stan's going to kill me when he finds out."

"Brosh, you're gorgeous," Annie says. "If you, like, cut the carbs, you'd get *so* much more work."

If Nick is byeong jugo, yak junda, then Annie's the opposite: yak jugo, byeong junda.

"Says the girl who sucks on cancer sticks. I'll stick with my *carbs*, thanks."

Annie holds up her hands. "Don't kill the messenger," she says. "You know how this business is."

The sad thing is, we both know she's right.

Annie scratches the stiff, starched Peter Pan collar of her gingham dress. "Nice outfit, by the way," I say.

Annie sighs. "Ugh. Nick's producing this new show, and my team wants me to make nice with him so he'll consider me for a part. *Must stay in character!*"

Must stay in character was what Nick always used to tell us on set.

"You're tired of playing ten-year-olds. I'm tired of playing to type, too," I say. "Why do we keep putting ourselves through this . . . this . . ." I'm grasping for the right metaphor. *Hamster wheel? Sausage factory?*

Annie finishes my thought. "Torture?" she offers, laughing. "Brosh, you say that *every* time you have a bad audition."

"I'm serious. If you didn't have to do this"—I point at her Perky Freckles outfit—"what *would* you do?"

"Get real, Brosh," Annie says. "I can't afford to fantasize—"

She stops abruptly. Nick beckons at Annie from across the room.

"Ugh, I gotta go kiss the ring," she says. "Hang in there, Brosh. I'm sure something will turn up. It always does."

6

PILOT SEASON

If you, like, cut the carbs, you'd get so *much more work.*

It should be that easy, right? If I want to be camera-ready, I need to lose the weight. If you want something badly enough, you make it happen.

Once upon a time, I *did* want it badly enough.

After I got fired from *Jump! Rope! Jungle!*, I despaired. There was now no denying my body. My career depended on me looking like a little girl. But seemingly overnight, I became a woman—with too much meat on her bones. I hated my reflection in the mirror, which was all curves and undulations. I'd never land an audition with this body, let alone a callback. I kept losing roles to girls who couldn't act their way out of a trash bag, but what did the CDs care, so long as they were skinny and cute?

A year after my *Jump! Rope!* failure, Stan wanted me to audition for pilot season. That's like college admissions for actors: You "apply" to a bunch of different TV shows, and if you're lucky enough, one of them will get greenlit to go on air.

The stakes were so much higher now than when I was a kid. Because I'd be competing with eighteen- and twenty- and even *thirty*-year-olds for the same "teen" roles. (Only I came with pesky child labor laws.) I was already reeling from the humiliation of getting fired. I swore I'd make myself "camera-ready," *no matter what.*

It started as a game.

I'd set my calorie limits for the day, and each day I'd try to beat the previous day's numbers. My diet consisted of poached chicken breast and raw kale, with vinegar and a stingy splash of olive oil. I cut out *all* carbs. I once "cheated" and ate a banana, and my whole world came crashing down. As penance, I drank only green juice for the rest of the week. By the end of it, my eyeballs were swimming in chlorophyll.

It was a weird time. I couldn't concentrate at all. All I could hear was the endless gnawing of my stomach, like it was trying to eat itself alive. I'd lie awake at night with hunger. I was always cold. And, not to be gross, but I barely did number two.

I was exercising like crazy, too: a five-mile run in the morning, then a HIIT workout, then Pilates, then cross-training with spin or swimming in the afternoon. This was on top of dance classes (and acting, and singing).

Then I stopped getting my period.

I shrank down to a size zero and got all the compliments:

You're so pretty now!

You're so healthy!

You just needed a little willpower!

But I still couldn't stand my body. I kept seeing myself

through the eyes of CDs, directors, producers, showrunners, and other actors: zooming in on my still-flabby arms or my too-big thighs. So I worked even harder to torch the fat. I'd see people chowing down on McDonald's or Shake Shack and feel morally superior to them. I finally understood when Kate Moss infamously said, *Nothing tastes as good as skinny feels.*

My obsession with "getting healthy" became *un*healthy—toxic even.

I felt weak all the time: physically drained from the over-exercising and lack of proper nutrition, and mentally drained from counting every calorie down to the last macro. The night before a big audition for a major network sitcom, I felt so dizzy I fainted. I was standing at the top of the landing. It was a miracle I didn't fall down the stairs.

Pilot season came. I was up for a few roles: a nerdy scientist on a teen Sherlock reboot. A mathlete on *Karate Amigos*. At one promising callback, for *Cheerleaders vs. Wizards*, a network exec was passing by the dressing room while I was changing. She sized me up and said, "You know, if you just lost ten pounds, it'd *really* help us envision you for the role!"

I DON'T HAVE TEN POUNDS TO LOSE! I wanted to shout. She didn't care that I'd worked myself to the bone to drop down to a size zero. But what was I going to do, yell at a Suit for body-shaming me? Obviously not; I had to smile and thank her for her feedback. I still wasn't a double-0 or triple-0, so I wasn't good enough. Maybe I was *never* going to be good enough.

Pilot season went. I gained all the weight I had lost, and then some.

MOM DIDN'T KNOW ABOUT the weight loss *or* gain—it had happened so drastically over the period of a couple months. We were crashing with a random cousin of Mom's in LA, and Mom had to keep flying back and forth to New York. Ryan was going through some stuff, and Dad had just started a new job and couldn't get any time off.

I never told my parents about the unhealthy dieting, the dizzy spells, my lack of a period and sleep and all of it. I never told them what the network Suit had said to me. Mom already had a lot going on with Dad, and Ryan, and I didn't want to burden her with more drama. When pilot season was a bust, I moved home to New York. Shortly after, my parents announced their divorce.

Since pilot season two years ago, I've had a handful of auditions and the extra role on *Law & Order*. That's pretty much it.

These days, I try to be healthy 75 percent of the time with 25 percent forgiveness wiggle room. Because I know how unhealthy it was to try for 100 percent perfection. I jog around Calvary Cemetery, which isn't nothing—running past three million dead bodies is hardly a walk in the park. I do my stretching and breathing exercises. I'm mostly fine with my appearance.

But if I'm totally honest, it's hard not to feel down on myself sometimes, given my line of work. My body carries a little "extra," especially for an Asian girl, since we're "supposed" to be the size of a thimble. In a lineup with other UAFs, I stick out like a sore thumb. For all this talk of body diversity, no real change has *actually* happened in Hollywood. You're still expected to be thin. In fact, it's even gotten worse, with all the weight loss drugs.

I had to learn the hard way that the yo-yo dieting, just like that yo-yo way of thinking, was unhealthy for me on the inside *and* out. I vowed to myself I'd never return to that dark space again.

Even if that's what it takes to be "Hollywood-ready."

7

SHERLOCK

I'm leaving the *Jump! Rope!* party. I put in my obligatory face time for Stan, and nothing's keeping me here. I head for the exit—and that's when I smack into the warm, broad chest of Liam Sweet.

"Hey," he says.

"Hey," I say, disentangling myself from him. He smells like his signature scent of spicy cologne and leather.

"We have *got* to stop running into each other like this." There goes that playful smile, those dimples, those dark, dark brown eyes . . . But no. I'm not falling for this bullshit again. Liam Sweet is a hot British heartbreaker.

And he 100 percent knows it.

Is it possible to hate someone but also want to, ahem, jump their bones at the same time?

"Kraft macaroni called. They want their cheese back," I say, which is also cheesy but I'm trying to make a point.

Liam laughs. "God, I've missed you, Brosh."

"Just because you people invented the language doesn't mean you get to abuse it."

He laughs again.

Liam Sweet and I met auditioning for *Sherlock Jr.* He just oozes leading-man energy, and of course he landed the role of Sherlock. I lost the role of Watson, the nerdy budding forensic scientist (female, 14–20, open ethnicity), to Stacy Smith, the girl who's in that new Marvel movie. They went white because they couldn't have *two* "ethnics" playing the leads. Liam and I stayed in touch, and he became my first boyfriend. Until one day he decided he wasn't.

"I'm in town for a spell," Liam says. "I'm screen-testing for a part." Damn his stupid accent! His stupid, hot English accent that makes you think of tweed blazers and Jane Austen remakes.

Liam pauses because this is where I'm supposed to jump in with *What part?* But I'm not going to give him that satisfaction.

"Erm, it's a teen reboot of 007."

It's almost *too* perfect that Liam Sweet would play James Bond.

I play it cool. "Good for you."

"Yeah, erm . . ." Liam runs his hands through his boyish flop of black hair. "Want to get out of here, Brosh?"

Liam Sweet is eye-candy clickbait. He should come with yellow *Hazard* tape. I should say no.

But I can't.

Maybe it's because I'm not the most confident person. I mean, I'm confident in my acting roles because I work hard on them, but when it's just me, I worry my light doesn't shine bright enough. If I'm next to someone whose light shines brighter, then maybe I feel it makes *me* shine brighter, too. Instead of being left in the dark.

In a weird way, I feel like if Liam wants to be with me, if he accepts me, then—by the transitive property—*Hollywood* accepts me.

So even though I know I shouldn't—*step away from the candy aisle, I repeat, step away from the candy aisle*—I say casually, "Sure. Why not?"

Liam and I exit, stage left.

Fade to black.

8

POMEGRANATE

I'm only five minutes late to meet Dad at Pomegranate the next morning, but he passive-aggressively checks his watch when I arrive. I can't help that track work makes the subways turn into spaghetti on the weekends. Or maybe I deliberately dragged my feet because I am dreading this breakfast so hard. Madame Olga, my old acting coach, would say that was my subconscious at work: *The body never lies, Broshka.* Because I have a feeling Dad's "important" nine a.m. news is to announce he's getting married to his "lady friend," Nabi Yoon.

I wish Dad would just text me the news instead of subjecting all of us to an awkward, overpriced "brunch." Like, save the two-hundred-dollar check for rubbery eggs and just give Mom and me the cash, you know?

"Ambrosia, finally," Dad says, and embraces me. He's been calling me Brosh less and less since he's been with Nabi.

Nabi's in the booth across from Dad. She is all the checkboxes: beautiful, thin, perfect skin, perfect makeup, perfect manicure, and tastefully dressed in silk and cashmere. She even has an MBA from Columbia. Mom would die if she met Nabi IRL.

"Ambrosia, thank you for coming," Nabi says coolly, studying me. Liam and I were hanging out until late last night, so this morning I just threw on a whatever dress. The effect I was going for was *boho*, but from Nabi's side-eye, it's probably more like *hobo*.

Sitting next to Nabi is a girl who's maybe a couple years older than me.

"Ambrosia, I introduce you my daughter, Clarissa Dunaway." Nabi speaks simple English. Korean's her dominant language. "She is junior at Choate."

Clarissa stands up to greet me. She's tall and thin, with the shoulders-thrown-back posture of a debutante or polo player. Her hair, long and glossy like Nabi's, is a lighter shade of brown. She holds out her hand to greet me. It is limp and delicate, like the wing of a bird. I don't know if she wants me to shake it or kiss it.

What does she think she is, royalty?

I go for the handshake.

"And where do you go to school?" Clarissa asks.

"GDS," I say.

"I never heard of it," she says in a dismissive tone.

Dad says, "But not for long. Brosh might be starting Mansfield Prep in the fall, right?"

Here we go again.

Dad and Mom can't agree on my schooling for next year. Dad wants me to go to Mansfield, this snobby all-girls private school on the Upper East Side. But Mom really wants me to stay at GDS. I was interested in LaGuardia, which is public, but after I got in, I kind of ruled it out because I figured it'd be GDS all over again. Even though they *do* offer some pretty cool electives.

The whole school thing is messy, and complicated, and another reason why it sucks to be the kid of divorced parents.

"Let's sidebar about this," Dad says. Which is fine by me, even though I was supposed to decide, like, yesterday.

"Clarissa will apply to Columbia," Nabi says. "She has 4.0 GPA, 1560 SAT, and is lacrosse and field hockey captain."

"Umma," Clarissa says.

"You're a slam dunk, sweetie," Dad says.

Sweetie? I shoot Dad a look he pretends not to see. He busies himself with his coffee. When he was with Mom, he used to take it "regular": milk with two sugars. Now he drinks it black.

"Is that because of legacy?" I ask it innocently, because Madame Olga says there should be tension between the dialogue and the tone it's delivered in. Also, it softens the burn. "Hey, it worked for George *Dubya*."

"Ambrosia," Dad says.

"The Bushes went to *Yale*," Clarissa says.

Okay, Choate. I almost say it aloud, but nunchi tells me not to. Nunchi is this Korean thing where you should have the sense not to do something socially clueless or whatever.

"Now we are all here . . ." Nabi nudges Dad, who clears his throat.

"Yes. We've gathered you here today because we have an important announcement," he starts. "Nabi and I—"

"You're getting married," I interrupt.

Nabi lifts her water glass to her lips, clearly upset I've burst their bubble. Dad says, "You could have let us have our moment, Ambrosia. You could have let *Nabi* have her moment."

"Sorry, but Nabi's diamond did all the talking." I nod at the silver band on Nabi's ring finger, with the diamond twisted inward. Mom used to do that with her ring while riding the subway.

"Umma!" Clarissa squeals. "Oh my God, let's see it!"

Nabi fake-blushes, then spins the ring around her finger so the diamond obnoxiously winks at us. Clarissa oohs and aahs. I flag down the waiter and order a Bloody Mary.

The server waits for Dad's approval. Dad shakes his head. *No.*

"Fine," I say. "A virgin Mary."

Everyone else orders champagne. Even Clarissa, because I guess she's a junior? Dad says they're planning the wedding for the end of the summer, before Clarissa returns to Choate. It burns me a little—okay, a lot—that my own father cares so much about *her* life, when, hello! Daughter #1 is right over here.

I reach for my phone to text Liam:

last night was fun

excited for JK tonight!

Liam invited me to be his "date" to Josie Kang tonight, because of course he also got tickets to her sold-out show. It touched me that he remembered I'm Kang Gang. But that was too corny and clingy to say to him aloud, so I joked, "I guess it pays to be a Sherlock."

Liam doesn't write back.

"Brosh. Brosh!" Dad says. I look up from my phone. "Ambrosia, Nabi has something she'd like to ask you."

Nabi clears her throat. "Will you girls be my bridesmaids?"

"Oh, of *course*!" Clarissa says.

"Oh," I say.

Dad turns to me. "Nabi thought it was important to make you feel like part of the wedding. And you girls are too old to be flower girls, ha-ha!"

This feels . . . weird. *Wrong.* I'm supposed to be the bridesmaid of the woman who's replacing Mom? But they're all staring at me expectantly, and what choice do I have but to mumble *okay*?

Thank God the waiter comes with our drinks.

We toast to the new couple. The virgin Bloody Mary burns my throat, and tears spring to my eyes. But I'll take that Tabasco sting over whatever I'm feeling now. How's Mom going to react when I break the news to her? She will flip. She will absolutely lose her mind.

Then I realize: We're meeting IRL because Dad wants *me* to be the one to break the news to Mom. To soften the blow for her, like I'm their mediator or something.

Dad made a killing in crypto—but only *after* he finalized the divorce from Mom. So alimony and child support were already set based on his pre-cryptonaire income. Mom doesn't know the half of it, but the half she does know makes her *pissed.* I always have to downplay how nice Dad's apartment is—2BR, West 50s, view of the Hudson River—so she won't feel more resentful than she already does.

"Did you tell Ryan?" I ask Dad, but he shakes his head.

"I tried calling him, but you know your brother. He's . . . flaky."

Ryan is backpacking in Southeast Asia, aka shutting all of us—especially me—out. His way of dealing with our family is by *not* dealing with us.

Liam finally texts a thumbs-up. At least there's that.

The waiter comes by again, and in addition to my overpriced egg entrée ($35), I also order all the things. As a small retaliation for having this breakfast foisted on me, I get:

-the bread-and-pastry basket ($29)
-a side of pommes frites ($15)
-an extra side of hash ($13)

"You're very hungry today, Ambrosia," Nabi murmurs.

"Don't worry, I won't tell your mom," Dad says, fake-conspiratorially. Which I guess is a joke about how Mom must make me watch my carbs because I'm an actor, and actors are supposed to watch their weight? But that's what Dad does; he tells dad jokes when he's anxious. The irony being *he's* the one who created this anxious situation in the first place.

"Don't worry, I won't tell Mom, either," I say. Dad frowns, not getting it. "Meaning, I'm not breaking *your* news to Mom."

Nabi plays the smoother-over. "Of course, Ambrosia. We just want to share good news with you first."

"Dad," I say, ignoring Nabi, "you realize you're putting me in an awkward position, right? Mom's going to ask me what this breakfast was about. And if I tell her, then she'll kill the messenger. But if I don't tell Mom and wait for *you* to tell her, then she'll kill me for *not* being the messenger. Either way, *I'm* the one dealing with the fallout!"

Dad goes, "Ambrosia—"

"No, Dad, *you* deal with it! *Today*, before I get home. I'm done being your go-between."

"Brosh, can't you act happy for us?" Finally, Dad calls me Brosh. But it's for all the wrong reasons.

"I'm off the clock," I say.

"Ambrosia," Dad says, "you're being dramatic."

As if to prove his point, I exit, stage left, to the restroom.

My arms shake as I clench the sides of the sink. Something about being around Dad—it gets my blood boiling. I've always been able to check my emotional baggage at the door when I'm on set, but the second the camera stops rolling, all bets are off. Everything I've been holding back, feelings-wise, comes pouring out. First, Dad abandoned Mom. Now he's abandoning me.

Madame Olga used to make us do this cruel exercise where you had to stay stoic while the rest of the class hurled jokes at you. If you cracked, you had to run a lap around the studio.

"Sometimes you must show *nothing* even if you feel *everything* inside," she'd said.

By the fourth lap, I had my poker face down pat.

I stare into the mirror and tell myself to keep it together. I make my face transform into a blank, indifferent slate—before I return to the scene.

9

MEET-CUTE

EXT. EYRE THEATRE – SATURDAY NIGHT

BROSH waits on line under the "Josie Kang Tonight! SOLD OUT" marquee. She checks her phone: nothing. Liam's still a no-show. Brosh sighs.

STRANGER
That excited to see Josie Kang, huh?

Standing behind Brosh is a STRANGER (teenage boy, a dead ringer for a K-pop idol, but with nerdier, real-life energy).

BROSH
(coming to)
Oh, that wasn't—I mean, I'm waiting for someone—
(off the Stranger's bemused look)
Are you *questioning* my Kang Gang loyalty?

STRANGER

You look like a sorority girl who discovered Josie Kang on *Instagram*, like, yesterday.

BROSH

(with mock horror)

What about me screams "Delta Kappa Gamma!"?

(beat)

Also, who's on Instagram anymore?

The Stranger cocks his head, sizing Brosh up. Does he like what he sees?

STRANGER

Prove it.

BROSH

(in a thick Queens accent)

So I'm on a date with this guy, who's eyeballing me like I'm a goddamn punch card for Panda Express. "Buy ten, get one free!"

STRANGER

(clapping)

Not bad! I stand corrected.

The Stranger's staring at Brosh, big-time. Yup. He likes what he sees.

STRANGER

I'm Teddy, by the way.

BROSH

I'm Ambrosia. But I go by Brosh.

They shake hands.

TEDDY

Wait a minute. You look *so* familiar . . .

Brosh grows uncomfortable. But, like the pro she is, she shrugs like it's NBD.

BROSH

I get that a lot.

TEDDY

(snapping fingers)

You were Golly Jee from *Jump! Rope! Jungle!* You were the OG Jee!

BROSH

(in disbelief)

How did you know?

Teddy gives her a look like *Please*.

TEDDY

Asians can read other Asian faces. I always thought it was so weird they never explained why one day Jee was you and, the next day, she was played by some other random Korean girl!

(grins sheepishly)

Confession. I had the *biggest* crush on Jee.

BROSH

Which one?

Teddy smiles: *I'll never tell.*

BROSH (CONT'D)
So what's your claim to fame?

TEDDY
Literally?

Teddy holds up his phone.

CLOSE-UP of Teddy's profile page:

Teddy_X

Stand-Up Comic

Followers: 9,999

BROSH
(whistling)
Nice flex. You're one bot away from a five-digit following.

TEDDY
Don't even! As soon as I get a new follower, someone—or some*thing*—unfollows me.

BROSH
I'm not even on anything. My agent wants me to keep a "clean slate." You're way more famous than I am.

TEDDY
(under his breath)
Not famous enough.
(normal voice)

Don't sell yourself short, Brosh. You're on a *Jump! Rope! Jungle!* subreddit on conspiracy theories . . .

(off Brosh's look)

I think it got, like, ten upvotes?

BROSH

I'll take it. So you're a comedian? Impressive. Tell me a joke.

TEDDY

(scoffing)

I'm not going to perform for you, like some monkey.

(beat)

You'll just have to come to one of my shows.

BROSH

You'll just have to invite me.

They stare at each other like *Touché*.

Brosh's phone buzzes with a text from Liam:

Sorry love

Don't think I'll make it

Just emailed u the tkts

Have fun wo me

I'LL MAKE IT UP TO U!!

Brosh curses under her breath.

TEDDY

Are you, like, waiting for your boyfriend?

BROSH

(a little too quickly)

No!

(beat)

Just . . . a friend. Who apparently flaked on me.

TEDDY

Bummer. I'm sorry, Brosh.

The line surges ahead. Brosh moves forward, but Teddy hangs behind.

BROSH

Hey, where's your seat? Maybe we're near each other.

TEDDY

(blushing)

The show's sold out. I was kinda hoping to scalp tickets.

BROSH

Perfect! Then you can take my extra ticket.

(sensing Teddy's hesitation)

No pressure if you don't want to sit with me . . .

TEDDY

No! I mean yeah! Wait, are you sure? Let me pay you—

Teddy reaches for his wallet. Brosh waves him off.

BROSH

I got these tickets for free.

(a shadow falls across Brosh's face)

In fact, you'd be doing me a favor.

TEDDY

(reluctantly)

Okay, if you say so . . . But only if you'll let me treat you to coffee after?

(beat)

Unless you don't drink caffeine . . .

(aw-shucksily)

How 'bout a chocolate malt at the soda fountain?!

(shakes his head)

Wow, that *so* didn't land. Try again, Teddy.

BROSH

(laughing)

Split the difference and say a bubble tea?

TEDDY

Done and done.

They laugh at their corniness. Teddy holds open the door for Brosh. They disappear into the theater.

FADE TO BLACK.

10

TEN THOUSANDTH FOLLOWER

Over boba, Teddy and I gush about Josie Kang's show. Teddy prefers Josie's earlier, edgier jokes, but I love all her new material in the show, which feels raw and honest and personal. She opens up about her family drama and also Hollywood basically screwing her over.

Teddy and I are the same age—sixteen—but weirdly Teddy's a junior at Xavier (he skipped a grade), and I'm still a freshman (I had to repeat a grade because I missed so much school for acting). It's kind of uncanny.

I ask how Teddy got into stand-up comedy. "I was always the youngest and smallest kid in my grade. I got bullied like crazy," he confesses. "I couldn't fight with my fists, so . . . I had to learn to fight with my words." He smiles sheepishly. "Comebacks were my only defense."

I remember the time Ryan came home with a black eye but wouldn't say what happened. Like . . . he was bound under a weird code of silence? But I was too young to understand.

"Your childhood sounds rough," I say.

"Understatement of the night," Teddy says. "Throw a bunch of boys together at recess, and it's like a prison yard."

"I hated school, too," I say. "I never made friends because my life was so different from the other kids. I was the only one working a nine-to-five." I laugh, trying to pass it off as a joke.

I don't talk about it much, but my childhood was lonely. I never made friends at school. They made fun of how I talked and acted—*You sound like a boomer!*—probably because I was surrounded by adult "coworkers" on set all day and I learned to imitate them. Some kids were jealous I was an actor, and they showed it in weird ways—like the mean girls pretending to save me a seat in the cafeteria, then icing me out the second I showed up with my lunch tray. I was always missing school for auditions and shoots, so teachers had to give me makeup work, which made *other* kids jealous that I was getting special treatment. And when I had to repeat the grade, it was beyond humiliating.

That's when Mom pulled me from my regular public school to a private theater school that was more accommodating of my work schedule. But at GDS, it became all about your creds. Film, TV, or streaming? Who was your studio and network? Which A-listers played your parents?

"Look at us," Teddy says. *"We're just a ragtag buncha misfits!"*

"Is that from something?" I ask.

"Never mind." He holds up his cup. "Cheers."

"Cheers."

I smile back at Teddy as I clink my cup to his. To be honest, we just . . . click. I barely met the guy, yet I feel like I can tell him everything.

It hasn't always been easy to talk to anyone about anything. It's not like I could spill my guts, when one wrong word could get me blacklisted by a director or a whole network. All my life, I've had to keep my mouth shut and my guard up. I was never free to speak. Even Annie and I can't tell each other everything; there's just too much on the line.

Last night, Liam started opening up about his feelings. Out of nowhere, he was all, "Fuck the studio! Let's, like, run away together, Brosh." And I'd said sarcastically, "Yeah, *okay*," but Liam went on and on, planning our exile to a little cottage in the Cotswolds, where we'd tend sheep and leave the business far, far behind. "You'd be a *very* fetching shepherdess, Ambrosia Lee."

When the future James Bond says a line like that to you, how can you *not* fall for it?

A nanosecond later, it was like a flip switched on (or off?) inside him, and Liam was all, "No, yeah, no, I *love* my producing partners. They're *really, really, really* good to me. I'm *so* grateful." I could feel the wall going up, the chains locking around his heart.

I take a long sip of my boba. "Josie Kang was so brave up there, spilling the tea about Hollywood," I say. "I wish *I* could just get up there and, like, speak my truth."

"What's stopping you?" Teddy asks.

"Uh, everything?"

"I'm serious," he says. "Brosh, you're a performer. Getting onstage is probably like riding a bicycle for you."

"For one, I don't know the first thing about writing a joke," I say. "A chicken, a podiatrist, and a nun walk into a bar . . ."

"Or maybe try flipping the order, so you start normal and end with the absurd?" Teddy suggests.

"See?" I say. "I'm not a comedy writer. I'm just an actor, and we're supposed to stick to the script. And these scripts, my God, Teddy! They're terrible. Every role is Unidentified Asian Female. You're just . . . boiled down to your 'type.'"

And suddenly I find myself trauma-dumping on Teddy. About getting fired from *Jump! Rope!*, about the roles drying up as I aged out, about not "looking the part." I do my best Stan the Agent impression, down to his thick New Jersey accent, as he's pitching me the E-Z Klean gig. I talk about the cringey audition and last night's cringey party.

But I stop short of telling Teddy about Liam. (Because nunchi.)

Teddy struggles to keep a straight face. "Sorry, Brosh," he says, "but that's all pretty funny. You could get so much mileage from the E-Z Klean bit alone."

"Yeah, my life's a total joke," I say sarcastically.

"No! That's not—I just mean . . ." Teddy looks at me helplessly, like he wants me to throw him a bone. "Brosh, you're basically sitting on a pile of comedy gold."

"*Gold* is not the first word I think of," I say. "Other piles, yeah."

"Comics take the *crap* in their life, pun intended, and spin it into a funny story," Teddy says. "What do you think Josie Kang did? She mined her 'trauma'"—he crunches his fingers into air quotes—"for laughs."

"Is that what *you* do with your stand-up?" I ask. "Tell tragicomic stories?"

"Hell's no," Teddy says. "I'm an observational comic. Like Seinfeld, only *actually* funny."

He pulls a leather-bound notebook from his pocket. "I carry this around everywhere since I started stand-up last year. I jot ideas, snippets of dialogue, descriptions of things I see on the street, whatever."

"But I thought comics just get up on the mic and, like, talk off the top of their head."

"That's what they want you to believe," Teddy explains. "But in reality, comics spend months, even years, writing and rehearsing their jokes."

I mimic my mind being blown. "So how do you even *start* writing a joke?"

"I start with something small and stupid that pisses me off," he says. "Like . . . avocados. Do you know Sheng Wang?" I shake my head no. "Well, he has this great bit about them."

Teddy pulls up the clip. A comic is nervously pacing the stage, like he just got bad news.

SHENG WANG

I'm sorry, I'm a little
stressed out.

(beat)

I . . . found out I got too
many ripe avocados.

I burst into laughter. I can't explain why exactly. I think because Sheng was setting it up like he was going to deliver devastating news: *My dog died. I failed the MCAT. My house is on fire.* And—twist—it's about something, as Teddy put it, "small and stupid."

SHENG WANG (CONT'D)
You find one ripe avocado,
that's a moment of *joy*.
You find a bag of five . . .
that's a *crisis*.

Sheng Wang's joke almost sounds like a poem.

"The comedy comes from the misdirection and exaggeration," Teddy explains. "Sheng Wang makes you *think* he's talking about a matter of life or death—but it ends up being something small potatoes, er, avocados. It's like comic exaggeration between his attitude about something and the thing itself."

I nod, getting it. "My old acting coach used to talk about stakes and 'subtext.' She said there's a power in doing the opposite of what the audience expects. Like, giving an understated delivery when you get bad news."

"Exactly!" Teddy says. He opens his notebook to a new page and shows it to me. "I actually do a stakes exercise to try to brainstorm more jokes. So say you have righteous anger about a ripe avocado, but you're totally chill about, like, a cancer diagnosis."

Low Stakes	High Stakes
e.g., ripe avocados	e.g., cancer. Like my grandma's diagnosis.
Bus is 2 minutes late	Death. Grandma's funeral. First time I ever saw my dad cry.
Missed a button on my shirt	Flunking out of school. Which, according to my dad, is getting a 95% on an AP Bio test.
Forgot to check the mail	Getting dumped by the hottest girl at school, because—surprise!—she was only pretending to like you to make her ex-boyfriend jealous.
Cashier didn't say hi	Never getting your dad's approval

I feel a little weird reading Teddy's journal, like I'm crawling through his mind and seeing all his private thoughts. I slide the journal over to him. "I hope you're not *all talk, no action*," I say. "Because one of these days, I just might come to see one of your shows."

"Oh, you *just might*?"

Did I just shamelessly invite myself to one of Teddy's shows? I sound *so* try-hard. "I mean . . . whatever! Or not," I sputter.

God, I have zero game.

"I'm doing a show tomorrow if you're free. I can put you

on the list. It's the least I can do for, you know, letting me be your date tonight?" Teddy suddenly blushes. "I mean . . . whatever! Or not."

"Now you're just making fun of me!" I say.

"Maybe, maybe not."

And Teddy breaks into a huge, boyish grin. It's the grin of someone who's never been told to rehearse it again and again for the hundredth take. It's infectious. And suddenly *I'm* smiling, too, like I'm doing it for the first time.

I haven't smiled like this in a long time—maybe even *ever.*

WHEN I GET HOME, I find Teddy's profile under my fake account so I can low-key stalk him. No wonder he has so many followers—his clips are funny and earnest and self-deprecating. Like he has this one bit about going on a first date with this girl, but as soon as she learned he was paying, she invited her whole family—parents, aunts, uncles, cousins. He's doing a lot of crowd work, calling on different members of the audience.

It's too bad the lighting's not great in his videos. Teddy's actually way more handsome in person. I wish the spotlight would catch his eyes and his cheekbones, but he's hooded in the shadows. That's actually a big problem in Hollywood. No one knows how to light Asian faces.

Teddy's posted a selfie from Josie Kang's show last night. I remember when he took it; we were squashed together in the cramped seats, knees touching. My face didn't make it into Teddy's selfie, but a sliver of my thigh did.

I take it as a sign. I hit follow before I lose my nerve.

I am now the ten thousandth follower of Teddy_X. He'll finally hit his five digits. He immediately sends me a DM:

Please tell me you aren't a bot

I DM back:

You know what they say.

You always remember your 10,000th.

He writes:

And you always remember your first.

Teddy_X hits follow.

OGGJ_Qns
Followers: 1 Following: 1

11

ACTING JOURNAL

Madame Olga used to make us keep an acting journal. "This will be your character dossiers," she said, holding up her own notebook. "You never know when you must play little girl from Kansas or old waitress from Manhattan and everything in between. An actor must always understand their backstory. Go to the street, observe, record! Be ready, always."

The morning after Josie's show, I pore through my old notes.

> M15. Old woman gets on bus with a granny cart. She hoists that thing up like it's light as a feather. Seems frail but surprisingly strong. She looks old, but her hands are smooth and wrinkle-free. What's the story behind those hands?
>
> 7 train. Guy in his 20s has red eyes and nose, jaw clenched. Slumps in his seat. Must have gotten bad news.
>
> Broadway and 9th Street. Teenage girl laughs into her phone. "That's the last time I do a short king!"

F train. Middle-aged woman carries her huge dog . . . in an IKEA BAG?? Okay, lady. Good luck with that.

I think about Teddy taking notes in his comedy journal all over the city. He said to start with something that pisses you off. I write:

Fake people
Toxic exes
Bad scripts
Double standards
Doppelgängers
Replacements

But . . . where's the humor? Everything's so vague. I remember one of my favorite Josie Kang jokes called "Bad Dates." It was the same joke I tried to tell Teddy when we first met. I find an early version of the clip:

"I went on a date with this guy. He's like, 'You're my third Asian.' He stares at me like I'm a coupon for the Wok N' Roll. 'Buy one, get a free chicken chow fun roll!' Give me a break, I'm not even Chinese!"

I transcribe the joke. It's actually not as funny on paper. And it's clunkier than later versions of the same joke. The humor comes from Josie's delivery: her physical comedy, her imitations or "act-outs" (surfer-dude voice for the date, an upbeat sales lady for the punch card), her facial expressions, and her committing to the bit. She actually gets on the floor and rolls herself up like a "chicken chow fun roll," whatever that is, and it's the most hilarious thing to watch. There are actually a bunch of different versions of the joke over the years, like Josie's still workshopping her material: In some, she says she's a "crab rangoon" or a "wonton burrito," or she's at the Panda Express instead of Wok N' Roll.

I keep writing, trying to come up with specific examples of things that irritate me:

Fake People

They have fake-ass voices, like they're on sleep meds but also sucked in too much helium.

They wear fake perfume that smells like flowers.

NOPE, too obvious. Like melted Jolly Ranchers? Candy canes?

What flavor? Is green apple funnier than peppermint?

Comedians are always talking about "misdirection" or the "twist" in a joke. Like Sheng Wang's fake stress!! . . . over avocados. What if I combined something sweet-smelling with something rotten? Like:

Rose petals and . . . NYC garbage stewing on the hot sidewalk in July? In a hot black trash bag on the asphalt? What's inside the garbage? Fish? Moldy fruit?

Lilies?

Water lilies?

Monet?

The Met?

Mom said Dad took her there on their first date

Or was it MoMA

Arggh

I draw a huge X through everything I wrote and start over again.

12

STICK OR COW

"Riddle me this: Why did I get a call from a certain casting director, over THE WEEKEND, telling me one of my actors went SEVERELY off script?"

Stan's face looms large on the computer screen. He never video-conferences with us unless it's to deliver really good or really bad news. Why Zoom when a phone call would do? Or, better yet, an email dictated to and dashed off by his assistant? And certainly not on a Sunday.

I've been dreading this inevitable call. I know I messed up, big-time.

"Brosh?" Mom says, waiting for an explanation.

"I . . . made a bad joke," I say. "I'm so sorry, Stan. I know this reflects badly on you."

My agent has every right to be pissed off at me. But Stan seems more confused than angry. I'm always the "good girl" on set: the non-complainer, the keep-my-head-downer. Only the superstars get to act like divas—throwing temper tantrums or showing up late to shoots, and the rest of the crew just has to take it. Yet in interviews, A-listers always *act* like they're so down-to-earth.

It's the fakest thing ever.

"Broshie, Broshie, Broshie." Stan shakes his head. "I don't think you understand what's at STAKE here. If you're going to go nuclear, do me a favor and give me a heads-up first? I damn near had a heart attack when I got the call from Carol! My Broshie? Pulling something like this? My pills were all the way in the other room, the doc's got me on these statins, don't even GET ME STARTED."

"I'm sorry," I say again. "But I couldn't take it, Stan. The CD and director were making comments about my body like I wasn't even there. *During* my performance."

"Did you forget and leave your big-girl pants at home?"

"Brosh," Mom asks, "what did they say?"

"They said I wasn't the right *look*." But I don't want to get into it because then Mom will go on her whole tirade again about Gwyneth Paltrow and The Chip.

Usually Stan laughs along with my jokes, which I crack when there's way too much tension in the room. But today he's not laughing along. "Brosh, part of the job is not just playing the part. It's *looking* the part."

"What about body diversity?" I argue.

Stan makes a farting sound with his mouth. "That's just PR. Hollywood's not diversifying a damn *thing*."

He stares me straight in the eyes. "Actually, Broshie, we can't put off this discussion anymore. The roles aren't exactly coming your way. *You* have to come to the role. We've been over this before. You have to ask yourself, 'Am I doing everything in my power to be Hollywood-ready? Am I willing to—'"

"Lose twenty or gain a hundred?" I snap.

Stan spreads his hands like *Eh . . . you said it, not me.* "You know how this industry works. I don't make the rules." He sighs. "What happened to you, Broshie? You used to be so hungry for it."

"Pun intended?" I interject.

Stan ignores it. "You had *drive*. Like when I put you up for pilot season two years ago. You were looking the part, you were getting the callbacks. It kills me that you couldn't keep it up."

But it was killing me *to* keep it up.

I'm about to say that, but Mom cuts in. "Stan, what else is coming down the pipeline?"

"Well, there's that Chinatown period piece I told you about," Stan says. *Chinatown project?* I mouth to Mom, but she shakes her head. "Someone dropped out, so we could get Brosh in—"

"*Jade Opium*? Absolutely not!" Mom interrupts. "I already told you that material is *not* appropriate for Brosh." Her voice is full of desperation. "What about ABC?"

"Still no word," Stan says. "Cindy, it's a struggle just to get Brosh *commercial* work. Let alone a meaty role like that ABC gig. There's a TON of competition. Cindy . . . I'm afraid that's it. We're salmon swimming upstream."

Stan looks off to the upper corner of the screen, which he does whenever he's stalling for time. I know all his tells.

"How do I put this delicately . . . ?"

"Just say it," Mom and I say at exactly the same time.

"I can only keep on clients that are working as hard for the roles as I'm working for them," Stan goes on. "And, Broshie, you're not willing to do what it takes. We just don't have any more work for your . . . type."

"Wait, are you *dropping* us?" Mom asks.

"I'm not saying the door's closed," Stan hedges. I can hear the *but* in his voice. "It's been a good run, kid."

I'm not willing to do what it takes? I have no words.

"Stan, we could have dropped you at any point when Brosh was making all that money for you," Mom argues. "But we stuck by you. Does that loyalty mean *nothing*?"

It's like Mom's not just talking about Stan.

"Cindy, the situation's out of my hands." He fake-glances at his Rolex. "I'm late for my two o'clock. Gotta run."

And we end the Zoom.

But because Stan is technologically inept, he's still on the call, and I can hear him telling his assistant: "Send the termination contract to Ambrosia Lee, stat."

Mom just sits there, motionless, at the kitchen table.

"Mom, I know I shouldn't have gone off script during that audition. It was disrespectful and unprofessional. I'm sorry," I start. "But, like, Stan was just trying to find any excuse to drop me!"

Mom comes to. "It's not a sorry if you add a *but*."

"But—"

"That was *extremely* out of character for you, Brosh."

Mom's not wrong. But it's the *way* she says it—like I can only fit one role?—that sets me off.

"Well, maybe I'm tired of playing to type!"

She presses her lips into a tight line. "We don't have time to discuss this. Go get ready for Kun-Gomo-Halmoni's banquet."

Then she gets up from the kitchen table and goes into her bedroom, closing the door behind her.

13

BANQUET

I'm reeling from the call with Stan. And now I have to get ready for Forced Family Time. Today we're going to my cousin Caroline's house for a lunch banquet for my great-aunt who's visiting from Seoul. Aka The Notorious KGH.

Kun-Gomo-Halmoni means Your Mother's Father's Older Sister, because Korean has a million different words for *aunt*. The last time I saw KGH was in LA for pilot season—when I was at my unhealthy skinniest, which she had plenty of unhealthy compliments about.

I'm dreading this banquet because KGH and the other aunties will pit me against my cousin Caroline (well, second cousin once removed), comparing whose eyes are bigger and prettier, whose nose is bigger and uglier, and whose calves look more mu-dari (giant white radish legs).

My aunties' beauty standards are harsher than a Hollywood casting room's.

So I'm standing in front of my closet, futzing. Do I wear

what's more fashionable, or what's more flattering? I was going to wear my navy dress, which is both, but I forgot that at Dad's.

Right after *Jump! Rope!*, I would wear all black, all the time. Because all black was "slimming." I was trying to hide my body behind these dark and baggy clothes so no one could tell how much weight I'd gained or lost. Those black clothes still sag in the middle of my closet.

At the far end is a bright yellow dress that's still new with tags. The dress is like a burst of sunshine. I bought it in a brave moment, but I'm not actually brave enough to wear it in public.

Annie texts me:

Hey

Saw liam at jenettes party last night

ugh

Still thinks hes all that & a box of condoms

good thing u dumped him!!

So that explains why he ghosted me last night at Josie Kang's.

Also, I didn't technically dump him; he just did the slow fade, and I took the hint. He didn't have the dignity to dump me himself.

Screw this. I reach for the yellow dress.

I text Annie that I met someone else at Josie's show. She writes back:

YEAH BROSH

GO GET IT!!

Mom knocks on my door. "C'mon, Brosh, I don't want to be late." She comes into my room and spots me in my yellow dress. She shakes her head. "What happened to your blue dress?"

I was originally going to wear that—if it weren't hanging in the wrong closet. "It's at *Dad's*," I say.

"You can say it without the attitude."

"What's wrong with this?" I ask.

"It's a little . . . loud." Mom starts riffling through my closet. "Let's find something more demure." You'd think Mom, as a (former) fashion designer, would *like* clothes that are loud.

She makes me try on a frumpy white frilly blouse and a long black skirt that looks like it belongs on the set of a period piece. "Mom, it's giving Colonial Townswoman," I say.

"Good. Then it nails the brief," Mom says sarcastically. "Your role tonight is to be quiet and respectful to your elders. And don't mention Stan. Let's keep it nice and vague."

She's on her hands and knees with her sewing kit, pinning the hem of the skirt. Her tailoring talents are wasted on this earlier settler equivalent of an outfit. We stare at her handiwork in the mirror. The clothes feel hot and stiff and uncomfortable. Their only selling point is that they are slimming-ish. I sigh loudly.

"You know what, Brosh?" Mom says abruptly. "Wear

whatever you want. I was just trying to spare you the unwanted attention." She closes her sewing kit. "We're leaving in five."

The subtext of her tone is *Don't say I didn't tell you so.*

I GO WITH THE yellow dress because at this point I can't stand down. But as soon as we step inside Caroline's, I regret not listening to Mom. We're overwhelmed by aunts, uncles, and cousins, and I can see the disapproval of my "loud" dress in their eyes. Still, I bow, bow, bow to a random assortment of elders I'm not 100 percent sure how I'm related to. Everyone asks about Ryan, oh, he's still traveling in Southeast Asia? How they miss him, how handsome he is! Even if my brother weren't backpacking abroad—gap year 1 expanding now to gap year 2—he probably wouldn't have shown up because he doesn't do family functions if he can help it.

Caroline's mom says to Mom, "You should have come early to help!" and drags her into the kitchen. I'm left to fend for myself.

I feel a pinch on my arm. It's The Notorious KGH.

"Ambrosia-ya?"

"Annyeonghaseyo, Kun-Gomo-Halmoni." I greet KGH with the little Korean I know, dipping my head into a bow.

KGH says something in Korean I can't understand. But she says *everything* with her eyes—the way she sizes me up and shakes her head. It's the same face the E-Z Klean CD gave me when she said, "Too chubby."

KGH switches to English so I can understand the full impact of her insult. "You fat now! Too fat for TV!" She says it loudly and publicly in front of all the relatives, as if it could be any more humiliating. And . . . I'm right back in front of the casting table/firing squad.

But what else can I do but smile and bow to my elder?

Caroline comes up from the basement, carrying an empty bowl. "We're out of chips," she informs her mom.

"But we're eating dinner soon, Caroline-ah," her mom says.

No one says, *Caroline-ah, stop eating the shrimp chips! They're making you fat!* Because Caroline-ah is skinny. And I am considered Fat by Lee Family Standards.

"They're for the boys," Caroline says, and that's enough to send her mom to the cupboard for the big red-orange bag.

Caroline spots me. "Hey, Brosh. Whoa . . . that's bold." She means my dress.

KGH points at my cousin and says, "*Something-something* skinny."

Caroline responds to KGH in her perfect Korean. I catch two English words: *curvy* and *trend*. Then she gives me a *Don't worry, cuz. I got you* look.

KGH asks, *"Curvy?"*

"Curvy-ga . . ." Caroline explains—curving her hands into an hourglass and blowing up her cheeks like a chipmunk.

It takes every ounce of my acting training *not* to explode at her.

Caroline is so fake. No disrespect to the real ones, but there are a lot of fake "body positivity" allies. Or is it "body neutrality" now? I can't keep up. Every time I doomscroll online, there's a new debate. (Which is why I try to stay offline as much as humanly possible, which is humanly *im*possible.)

Then Caroline says to me, in English, "You know, Brosh, if you just lost ten pounds, okay, twenty, tops, Halmoni would get off your case. Also, dark colors are more slimming."

Why is it okay to tell someone to lose weight, but you can't tell them to lose ten pounds (okay, twenty, tops) of meanness?

"It's really not that hard, Brosh," Caroline goes on. "All you have to do is swap a big, yummy salad as your main meal for the day. There are *so* many recipes online! Sometimes I just skip a meal when I'm not feeling, like, super hungry."

And now she's dietsplaining me? I already eat healthy and exercise regularly; I don't need her "health" advice.

So I channel my best Josie Kang. "You only got into Binghamton when your sister got into Cornell? It's *really* not that hard, Caroline. All you had to do was study harder!"

And it works—I've hit Caroline where it stings. But when I see the hurt flooding over her face, it doesn't feel as good as I thought it would.

It kind of makes me feel like a jerk.

AFTER LUNCH, MOM IS in the kitchen, cleaning up. I'm about to go in and offer to help, but KGH says something to Mom. I catch the word ssaljjusseo: *fat*. Which is pretty messed up that it's one of the few Korean words I know.

Mom just lowers her head and says, "Nae." *Yes.*

KGH won't let up. "Cindy-ya!" she says. "*Something some-*

thing . . . Ryan-Appa." So now I know KGH is talking about Dad. And the way KGH pinches Mom's stomach and then flings her arm, I know exactly what she's saying—*You chased him away.*

Mom doesn't defend herself. She just bows her head deeper and takes it.

It kills me to watch KGH bullying Mom. I'm filled with so much righteous anger—han?—on my mother's behalf. Before I can stop myself, I shout, "Leave Mom alone, Kun-Gomo-Halmoni!"

The scene stops. KGH glowers at me. But she's not the one who yells at me; it's *Mom*.

"Brosh, how *dare* you speak to an elder like that? Say you're sorry, *right now*!" Mom bows her head, low, to KGH. "죄송해요 큰고모. 너무 죄송해요 . . ."

I swear Mom's about to push my head into a bow, too. She wants me to repeat after her. But I don't know the lines. Even if I did, I won't be forced into an apology.

Kun-Gomo-Halmoni fixes her eyes on Mom, then me.

"똑 닮았네 . . ."

I don't know what the words mean.

But I can tell Mom gets exactly what KGH is putting down.

14

TIME AND PLACE

"I don't even know where to *start* with you!" Mom says when we get home from the banquet. "First the audition. Then Stan. Now Kun-Gomo-Halmoni? I can't even *begin* to express how *disappointed* I am with you, Ambrosia."

"Yeah, but she was being a bully!" I argue.

"Have some empathy," Mom says. "Your Kun-Gomo-Halmoni is from a different generation. And she's your elder!"

"More like *elder abuse*."

"That's not funny," Mom says hotly. "You're developing a real attitude lately. You think you can just mouth off about anything that bothers you? You're almost an adult, Ambrosia. It's time to grow up!"

Mom just passively lets things happen, and I can't take it anymore. "Well, maybe I'm making up for lost time!" I cry. "You never stand up to anyone—not to Kun-Gomo-Halmoni, not to Stan, not even to anyone at *Jump! Rope!* Mom, grow a backbone!"

Mom presses her lips into a tight, angry line. "Brosh, there is a *time and place* to speak out."

"Yeah, like never," I mutter.

"What was that?" Mom asks sharply. It's a rhetorical question, so I don't answer it. She sighs. "Brosh, I *never* forced you to do anything you did not want to."

She's right, on a technicality. *I* was the one who was first interested in acting. When I first started in "the biz," I was a catalog model. But I was tired of just standing there with my hand on my hip, being told to "smile and look cute!" Some of the other kid models I'd meet at shoots were also taking acting classes, and I asked Mom and Dad to sign me up. Playing make-believe was way more fun than standing around in stiff clothes and doing awkward poses and never uttering a word. It felt like the difference between Technicolor vs. black and white.

For the record, my parents never pushed me.

"You had opportunities other girls could never dream of. And now you're throwing it away with these *antics*?" Mom says. "When I was growing up, we had zero representation on TV or in movies. Brosh, you have the chance to make history."

"With what?" I ask. "*Look, Ma! It's getting whiter!*?"

"You're an actor, not a comedian," Mom snaps. "Save it for your stand-up routine."

Her phone rings. "Hello, Tim," she answers. "No, as good a time as any . . ."

Oh great, it's Dad. His timing couldn't be any worse. In fact, it's comically bad.

He's saying something on the other line. Breaking the news, presumably.

Mom grips the phone, her knuckles white. The room feels *so* small. There's not enough air. Mom's a puddle of self-pity. I just can't.

My phone pings.

Hey my comedy shows at 5

Hope u can make it

I put u on the list!

It's from Teddy.

"Where do you think you're going?" Mom demands.

"Taking you up on your other suggestion."

And I grab my bag and haul out of the house *so* fast, before Mom can slip down into a funk and I'm the only family member around to pick up the slack.

15

JESTER'S PRIVILEGE

On the train ride to Teddy's show, I'm hit with the full impact of what went down: KGH. Mom. Stan. *Dad.* I grab my acting journal and start to free-write, my feelings angry and raw:

UGHHHHH who does Stan think he is, suddenly dumping me like I'm yesterday's garbage? He makes me feel SO worthless!

All those years I spent training and going to auditions and smiling big-big for the cam-cam . . .

For what?

For NOTHING!

You're so stupid, Brosh!

But . . . is STAN the one making me feel worthless?

Or is it society, media, the whole Hollywood Industrial Complex?

Am I hating the player, or the game? Or BOTH?

Showbiz Industrial Complex—SIC?

It's sick.

Most people don't have to worry about becoming a career failure until they're middle aged.

I got a head start in life. It happened to me at 14!

Ever feel like your career's on life support?

My agent pulled the plug on me.

Issued Do Not Resuscitate.

Pronounced me dead on the scene.

TEDDY'S PIN DROPS ME at a desolate alley on the Queens side of Brooklyn, or maybe it's the Brooklyn side of Queens? This can't be right. Google Maps must be drunk.

A sandwich board reads *Jester's Privilege*, with a chalk arrow pointing down a dark set of stairs. I get more sad-community-theater than serial-killer-lair vibes. I head down the narrow, steeply pitched steps, practically breaking my neck.

Damn. The depths I'll go for a crush, if not comedy.

I end up in a small basement performance space: Some folding chairs are set up to face the "stage"—a wooden pallet on the floor, with a lone microphone lying on top. The room is *painfully* empty. I'm having PTSD from this off-off-off-Broadway gig I did right after *Jump! Rope!* Most nights we'd perform to an empty basement theater. The gig was so small, Stan just handed it off to Sadiya, one of his two assistants at the time. On a "good" night, there'd be a handful of tourists, pissed off that *The Lion King* was sold out. Their faces and crossed arms told me everything: *Synesthesia: All the Colors You Can Smell!* was no Simba & Co.

I feel a tap on my shoulder—Teddy.

"Brosh, I can't believe you actually made it!"

"You kidding? I wasn't going to miss this," I say.

Teddy blushes. "Hey, I'm sorry it's so . . ." He gestures around the empty room. "A lot of people *said* they were going to come, but . . ."

He trails off again.

"People suck," I say sympathetically.

"Appreciate you," Teddy says.

"Oh! I took your advice and started jotting some notes." I grab my acting notebook and show it to him.

"There's some good stuff here," Teddy says, flipping through the pages. "Like I said, you should get on the mic sometime."

Yeah, right. That's what the me from yesterday would have said. But yesterday me didn't fight with Mom, talk back to KGH, get dumped by Stan, and end my career.

"I just might," I tell Teddy.

"I've got to say hi to the other performers in the 'greenroom.'" Teddy curls his fingers into air quotes. "Thanks again for coming, Brosh."

"Break a leg, Teddy! I mean, not literally. Those stairs were *treacherous.* And most likely condemned."

Teddy smiles. "You have a very . . . interesting way of talking, Brosh. Anyone ever tell you that?"

"Only all the time."

I get that a lot: *You don't sound* normal. *You don't sound like a kid. You talk like a forty-year-old.* It's what happens when you're a kid with adult coworkers.

Teddy smiles at me, shy and hopeful, then disappears backstage behind the curtain.

The show starts. The host, Mike, says, "Welcome to the Jester's Privilege Comedy Hour! We've got a *packed* house tonight, folks!"

By *folks*, he means *me*. But I clap and whistle loudly, to make up for the fact that I'm the only one in the audience.

"Let's give it up for our first comic, Ben!"

Ben bounds onto the stage and fist-bumps Mike.

"Hey, so I'm working on some new jokes," Ben says. "Uh . . ."

He has a journal onstage with him, and he starts flipping through his notes. "You know what I hate the most? People who eat potato chips quietly. It's so annoying. Those people should be dragged into the street and shot! Make some noise if you agree."

Ben looks down at me, as if waiting for me to respond. I remember how lonely it is up onstage—even if the "stage" is a beat-up plank of wood. So I clap in performerly solidarity.

He seems relieved. "See? Even this chick agrees with me." He twists the cord of the mic, which creates a loud reverb. "Crap! I lost my train of thought."

As Ben flips through his notes, there is a long, dead, excruciating silence.

This is stand-up? More like a comedy of errors.

Ben is actually the most polished of the bunch. Every comic who goes up just riffs nonsense. The worst of them make cheap, hacky jokes. They scroll through their phone notes or shuffle the pages of their journals. Whole beats of silence go by as they try to remember where they left off. This "show" feels like a parody of a bad table read. *Never waste the audience's time.* That was always the golden rule in Hollywood.

It's Teddy's turn. He walks across the plank—stage—whatever—like he's leading with his chest? He pounds Mike's fist with his own and grasps the mic with . . . *swagger* is not quite the right word. Just before the show, Teddy seemed anxious and shy. Now he's carrying himself with a bolder, more confident energy. He starts his set.

TEDDY

I know what you're all
thinking:
Who's this scrawny Asian kid,
and why isn't he home studying
for the SATs?

Teddy onstage is funny, and fresh, and charming. I'm blown away—seeing this whole new side of him.

I was forced to go to hagwon.
That's Korean for "bloodsport
academy."
Instead of spit buckets and
boxing gloves, we get Scantrons
and number-two pencils.
We're all thrown into the ring,
Trying to KO—
on math and verbal.
We're duking it out for the *one
spot* at Harvard
reserved for *all* the Asian
people.
Give it up for quotas!

As his set goes on, some of the lines land; some don't, if I'm being honest. If I'm being *honest* honest, I think Teddy's stage presence could use some work. His delivery is at times awkward, and sometimes he muffles his lines, like he hasn't fully committed to them. There are good breathing techniques and movement exercises he could do. And when his jokes don't land, Teddy turtles his shoulders, instead of lifting his chest. I don't think he realizes it. I know some of it's nerves. But he's still way above the other comics.

I kind of can't believe it. Teddy_X is just owning it on the stage.

THE LAST COMIC SEEMS to be a no-show. Mike says, "Is there a Joe in the house? Last call. Going once, going twice . . ."

It's been amateur night all night. Honestly, all the other comics except Teddy sucked. If they can do it, why can't I?

Dance like nobody's watching. Josie Kang said that once in an interview. The second you stop caring about what other people think, you're free to do your own thing.

And suddenly I'm raising my hand. "I'll take his slot."

Mike shrugs. "Sure, I guess," and hands me the mic.

What am I doing?

Teddy's standing in the back row. I shrug like *I guess I'm doing this?* He gives me a thumbs-up.

"Hi, good evening! Was it just me, or did anyone else get lost coming here? I don't know what's harder, finding Nemo, Narnia, or the Jester's Privilege!"

The joke falls from my mouth and lands, no exaggeration, with a thud. I can feel my cheeks getting flushed. Teddy nods encouragingly.

"Hey! Uh . . . I, uh, wow. It feels super weird to be up here. I've never done this before. And they say you always remember your first, right? But this is more . . . painful?"

Teddy guffaws.

"So I got dumped by my talent agent today. Give it up for me." I clap for myself, which is just the saddest thing ever. "Irv—not his real name—is such a cliché of a Hollywood agent: you know, boomer with a Jersey accent, a fake tan, a Rolls-Royce, and a fourth wife."

I actually have no idea what kind of car Stan drives. (Also, he's still on his second wife.) But it sounds funnier to exaggerate.

"Irv's like a used-car salesman who wishes he was selling Cadillacs instead of Honda Civics. All, 'Ayyy! Have I got a *car*—I mean a *role*—for you!'"

I point my fingers into air guns and do an over-the-top shoulder shimmy.

"Irv loves going to McDonald's—not for the Big Macs, but to scout for clients. He's all, 'Listen, sweetHAWT. You got the makings to play McDonald's Employee #1!'" I pinch my fingers into a viewfinder. "'I'll make some calls to the big head honchos in THE BIZ. Stick with me, kid! I'll make you a STAH!'"

It's such a bad joke, but Teddy flashes me another thumbs-up.

"Irv was all, *I love you, you're perfect, now change!* Whatever happened to *just be yourself*? Nah, that's the BS they sell us to keep the bumper sticker industry in business."

I take a deep breath. "It's all crap. They don't want us to *just be ourselves*. Not Hollywood, not Barbie, not any of it. They want you to play someone *else*. Because guess what, been there, done that. I tried to change myself, and it still wasn't enough! *Just be yourself*, my *ass*."

It feels so good to say my inner thoughts aloud. The things I've been feeling for half my life, ever since I started in the business, that I've bottled up inside for years.

I quickly come up with another impression:

"So . . . my last boyfriend was an actor. A real Hollywood type. Let's just call him . . . Holmes. Holmes was hot as hell but dumb as bricks. He's all, *Me so handsome! Everybody love me!*"

I throw my arms up into flexed biceps, and for some reason, I twirl on my tiptoes—like a ridiculous cross between a WWE wrestler and an Irish Riverdancer. I don't half-ass it, either; I fully commit to the bit.

"Holmes couldn't do two plus two to save his life, but damn, was he eye candy."

I'm losing Teddy. He's on his phone, typing. Is he texting someone else?

I drop the Liam act and do an impression of a ditzy Valley Girl actress type (The Other Jee). Teddy stops staring at his phone and starts laughing—like, *really* laughing—at my impression. Emboldened, I follow it up with an impression of a social-climbing trophy wife (Nabi). It's like I can't shut it off.

But it almost doesn't matter if Teddy laughs or not. I'm performing for myself. For the first time in my life, I'm not repeating rehearsed lines—lines written by somebody else.

And then Mike holds up his phone's flashlight in my face—my cue to wrap up.

"*Ayyy*, I'm here all night!" I curtsy, take a huge bow, and practically trip off the wooden pallet stage.

I feel such a *rush.* I was unscripted—free.

I have officially bombed my first open mic.

And I can't wait to go up again.

END OF ACT I.

Pizza

What's the deal with Domino's pizza?

It's like eating a bagel-flavored car tire. (???)

It's like the holy trinity of rubbery, flabby, and tough.

How can you try so hard to be so bad?

MTA

A manspreader on the train just made me spill my coffee all over me.

I swear I didn't soil myself.

How many years of our lives do we spend

waiting for the buses and trains?

Doctors could cure cancer

in the time it takes to wait for a stalled F train

stuck in Coney Island.

Want to solve world peace?

Get the MTA to run on time.

Exes

My ex posted pics on a beach in Ibiza

with a mysterious headless girl in a bikini.

I accidentally liked it.

And then I was like, "Oh, crap!" and I unliked it.

But now I was worried he'd see my unlike and think I wasn't over him—

so I "reliked" my "like" and added a comment: "You guys are SO cute!" just to double-down.

But THEN I worried I was being so "try hard."

So I'd have to post a pic of me and some other guy.

Problem is, there is no "other guy," so I photoshopped a pic of me and The Rock.

But then that seemed creepy, so I just disabled my account altogether.

I devoted 24 hours of brainpower to this first-world problem.

Cavemen are scratching their heads like "We invented <u>fire</u> and the <u>wheel</u> for this?"

OMG these jokes are <u>GARBAGE</u>!!!

Stakes Chart

Low Stakes	High Stakes
e.g., ripe avocados	e.g., cancer
	Mom & Dad's divorce
Maybe someday?	Career death
	Liam big-timing me
	Getting dropped by Stan

ACT II

COMEDY

Beauty is only skin deep—
but ugly goes clear to the bone.

—Dorothy Parker (allegedly)

16

STAND-UP CURIOUS

"Brosh, let me get this straight: You lose one little bleach gig, and now you suddenly decide to quit acting to become a comedian? *Have you lost your mind?*"

Annie's back in New York, and we're hanging out at a coffee shop near her loft in Brooklyn. She crosses her arms, waiting for an actual answer.

"I'm just . . . stand-up curious," I say. Ever since my first mic two weeks ago, I've been bitten by the comedy bug. I've been to a few mics since, and they went way better than the first. I mean—I'm still bombing, hard. But I'm learning to get more comfortable onstage. And Teddy's sent me a bunch of helpful how-to videos and podcasts. I'm planning to spend spring break this week performing every day.

"You're insane with a capital K," Annie goes on. "All those people, staring at you and *judging*? No thanks."

"Right," I say, "because no one's judging you at all the

auditions, callbacks, chemistry reads, and screen tests." I tick each item off my fingers. "At least now *I* get to be the one holding the mic."

So what if no one's listening.

"And the rush! Annie, it's like . . . it's like . . ." Words can't even. Everything around me starts to feel like a joke—literally.

The Q58 is delayed, again? Joke.

Manspreader on the M? Joke.

Nabi forcing me to watch her go try on wedding dresses this afternoon? Joke.

Liam posting pics from Ibiza with a mysterious sombrero'd girl in a hot-pink bikini, and me pretending not to be jealous? Joke.

Mom barely speaking to me ever since she got hit with the Stan-Banquet-Dad one-two-three punch?

Not a joke. That one hits too close to home.

"Enough about me," I say. "Let's talk about you." I nod at Annie's baseball cap, brunette wig, and sunglasses. "Who's styling you these days?"

It's hard for "America's sweetheart" to walk around in public without getting mobbed. Her "core base" is split between nine-year-old fangirls and creepy older dudes who probably live in their mom's basement.

"Brosh!" Annie shushes me. I squint around the coffee shop. Just a bunch of hunched-over millennials wasting time on their laptops. No paparazzi.

"Right. I'm sure *that* guy"—I nod in the direction of a dude blowing the schmutz from his earbuds—"is a total pap."

She's still whispering. *"You never know."*

We drink our overpriced lattes. "What's Cindy say?" Annie asks. "I can't see her signing off on this."

"She doesn't, like, *love* it."

That's a huge understatement. Mom and I actually got into a huge fight about it when I came home from my first mic and announced *this* was what I was going to do over spring break.

"I've been putting out feelers to other agents. We've worked so hard to keep you a nice clean slate. So now you want to run your mouth and sabotage your acting career?" Mom said, and *I* said, "What's left to sabotage? It's already DOA."

Eventually, Mom dropped the subject. Deep down, she knows she can't actually control whether or not I do stand-up. When you start earning your own paychecks at age eight, the standard parent-child playbook goes straight out the window. Plus I spend every other week at Dad's, anyway, and he's Switzerland on the matter. He thinks stand-up is just a "hobby."

Annie rolls her eyes. "What's the point of all this . . . funny business?" She laughs at her own joke. "First, stand-up. What's next, a Scientology cult? Brosh, you sound like a fucking addict! I should know. *Fuck.*"

Annie glances around again to make sure no one overhears her dropping f-bombs. Because Perky Freckles doesn't cuss. And Perky Freckles doesn't talk about her alcoholic mom.

I still remember Donna on set. She'd go from one extreme to the other—all bubbly smiles one minute, and then the next minute she'd be red-faced, tripping over camera wires and shouting at anyone who crossed her path. Annie was always apologizing for her mom, always baking cookies for the crew after another one of Donna's outbursts. "Brosh, you have, like, the perfect family," Annie would say to me. She still believes that, even after my parents' divorce.

At a certain point, Annie had to emancipate herself because Donna and her husband, Earl, were skimming off the top of Annie's earnings, and then some. Annie's team worked hard to keep the rehab and emancipation news hush-hush so it wouldn't tarnish her "America's Sweetheart" image.

"My manager's making me sign for another season of *Burn Off! Kidz*. And then they want me to do those kiddie Christmas specials." Annie makes a face. "Got to *protect the brand*! At this rate, I'll be playing ten-year-olds till I'm forty."

"What if you just walked away?" I ask. "You'd be comfortable enough living off your residuals, and your merch deals . . ."

Last I heard, the McDonald's Perky Freckles doll was going for ten grand on eBay.

"Please," Annie says. "You think my mortgages are going to pay themselves? Or Mom's rehab? What about my little sister and brothers, are they going to just *starve*? Oh, and Earl? You think he's just going to go away quietly without a payout?"

Annie owns three homes, and she's not even old enough to vote.

"I've got enough crap on my plate to deal with, Brosh," she goes on. "AI stealing my job? Footage of me getting leaked onto some pervy website? We don't even have basic protections in the business." She sighs. "But hey! As long as the check clears."

"Amen, I guess." We clink cups.

My phone pings with my calendar alert: I'm meeting Teddy at an open mic later. Annie goes, "*Ooh*. Hot date with your comedy guy?"

"Actually, Teddy and I are just meeting up to tell some jokes."

It's impossible to keep a straight face; I can feel myself breaking into a huge, sloppy grin.

"Look at you!" Annie gives my arm a playful slap. "So what's the deal with you guys? Are you, like . . . ?"

I right my face. Try. "Teddy and I are just . . . I don't know! He's so hard to read."

We've only hung out a few times. But as soon as I start to think Teddy *like* likes me—he does something totally friend zone.

"Girl, *you* need to make the first move," Annie says. "Guys are so clueless. Put that vibe out there!"

"I don't know . . ."

"Liam was *so* toxic, Brosh," Annie says. "I'm glad you found a new boy toy."

"He's not a *boy toy*—"

Annie's phone rings. "I got to go, too. My car's outside.

I've got this meeting with my lawyers. Want me to drop you off somewhere?"

"I'm good."

We hug goodbye on the street. Annie adjusts her wig under her baseball cap and pushes on her sunglasses, then slides into a black car with tinted windows and drives off.

17

FIRST IMPRESSIONS

An hour later, I'm onstage and bombing again. I'm first in the lineup at the Vault, which means I have to warm up a cold room.

"So, uh . . . anyone have Barbies growing up?" The answer's a resounding no.

Rookie mistake #433: Not knowing your audience.

Well, there goes that bit about Barbicide. Ryan and his best friend, Jimmy, used to think it was funny to steal my Barbies and decapitate them. I'd scream when I found blond plastic heads under my pillow or in my lunchbox. (To Ryan's credit, he did eventually stop hanging out with Jimmy because he was a total jerk.)

I try again. "I was recently accused of racism . . . by another Asian."

The punch line gets a *slight* chuckle—or maybe it's more like a throat clearing?

Now's probably not the time to insert a flashback, when

I'm dying alive a minute into my set. But ever since I ran into The Other Jee, I can't stop thinking about all those times we were thrown together in the same audition rooms. I was feeling anxious about this one role, which had a few lines in Korean, because my Korean sucks. Jee overheard me rehearsing the lines to myself and said, "I'm sure nobody can tell that you don't *actually* speak Korean, Ambrosia!"

The Other Jee totally psyched me out. In the audition, I forgot all my lines—Korean *and* English. The irony was that no one at the casting table knew Korean, anyway. I lost, and she won the part.

Pro tip: Never rehearse in the waiting room. There are too many saboteurs.

"So this *other* Asian told me *I* wasn't 'Asian enough,'" I say. "How do you *measure* Asianness? Is there a size chart? Like those tiny ones printed on your sneaker tongues? US women's size 7, which translates to UK size 5, which translates to French . . . baguette."

Crickets.

Maybe that joke was too corny or silly. Or racist? Great, watch the French cancel me over a bread joke.

"Hey, what's up with British measurements? Pence. Tuppence. Farthing. *Stones.* Stones? Who the heck measures their weight in *rocks*?"

I channel Liam and attempt a British accent: "Bollocks! Shouldn't have eaten that last crumpet, I gained five pebbles! Which translates to 4.8 ounces, which translates to 0.3

kilograms"—I just make up a number—"which actually translates back to 5.*1* pebbles, because something always gets lost in the conversion."

Speaking of getting lost, my .1 joke doesn't get a single laugh. Not even a *ha.*

Maybe this isn't a mathy crowd?

Or maybe the crowd is comatose.

The "audience" of other comics, mostly dudes, goes from not laughing to not even paying attention. They're on their phones or staring down at their notebooks. That's . . . rude.

"What's it take to get a perfect one hundred percent?" I commit to the bit, throwing my hands over my head like an Olympic gymnast about to get her perfect score.

Not even a clap.

Hello? Is this thing on?

I try to salvage my act by doing some over-the-top impressions of people I know, which manages to scare up a few laughs. Still, I bombed. Teddy offers me a sympathetic smile when I get off the stage. And of course, when *he* goes up, he kills it. He does a bit I saw him post about online dating and who pays for a first date, including an act-out for the "dance of the check at the end of the night"—which is really funny but, I'll admit, makes me feel a tiny pang of jealousy at whoever this mystery girl is.

The comic after Teddy starts telling the worst one-liners:

"Why do brides wear white? *So the dishwasher matches the kitchen!*"

There are a couple chortles. The comic, Jim, goes on:

"Why are boys smarter than girls? *Because we have two heads!*"

I groan. This guy is a total hack. I'm wondering if I should say something. But Teddy catches my eye. He shakes his head like *Forget it, he's not worth it.*

AFTER THE MIC, TEDDY asks if I want to grab coffee and work on our jokes. We head to Seoul Café in K-Town.

"I bombed. Again," I say.

"You were . . . fine," Teddy says.

I cover my face. "That's worse than bad!"

Teddy laughs. "At least no one threw an egg roll at you."

"Please tell me you're joking."

"Nope. Egg rolls, burritos, kebabs, you name it . . ." Teddy ticks the food projectiles off his fingers. "And I thought DEI was dead—hey, that line's not bad." He scribbles it down in his journal.

"People are the worst," I say.

"Totally. It took six months before I got my first laugh," Teddy says. "Can I give you some feedback? I mean, totally fine if you don't want it—"

"Shoot."

"Brosh, I think you kind of lost the crowd with the Barbie stuff. It was a roomful of dudes. It wasn't really a *doll* vibe."

"Because Barbies are dolls but Star Wars 'action figures' aren't?"

The guy before me did a whole bit on his childhood toys, which got laughs. But I kind of get Teddy's point: Know your audience. I wasn't connecting with them because they couldn't relate. That being said, I could name every one of Ryan's Star Wars, Marvel, and Transformers "dolls," but my brother couldn't tell the difference between Barbie and an American Girl.

"Right," I say. "It was more of a my-trad-wife-is-a-dishwasher vibe."

"Brosh, forget that guy. Everyone knows he's a hack," Teddy says. "Comedy's so lowest common denominator. It's, like, to get the whole room laughing, you have to speak to the dumbest people in the audience."

"*That's* dumb," I say.

"I liked your act-outs," Teddy says. "Those were so funny."

"They were fun to do, but it kind of felt like I was making fun of those people?" I shrug. It's hard to explain, but when I was imitating The Other Jee, or Nabi, or Liam, it felt fun in the moment, but at the same time, it also felt . . . mean?

"Isn't that the point?" Teddy says. "You were punching up."

I read that it's okay to "punch up" to people with more power. Like, it's okay to make jokes about politicians and billionaires, because in real life they have the power to crush a Nobody like you. So maybe Teddy's right. But the jokes still kind of left a bad taste in my mouth.

Teddy suggests we do a writing exercise: make a list of things people first notice about me.

"And don't go easy on yourself," he says. "Like, all the

non-flattering physical stuff, or anything people see or hear—or *smell*, ha-ha—when they first meet you."

"If I wanted a list of everything physically wrong with me, I'd go to a casting call. *Too fat, too old, not pretty enough,*" I say. "Teddy, it's comedy, not a beauty pageant."

Teddy raises his eyebrows. "You'd be surprised. They're not all that different."

"Where'd you learn to do this?" I ask. "On that Josh Rogaine podcast you sent me?"

"It's not called—"

"I know, I know, it's a joke."

Teddy takes a sip from his coffee. "Brosh, you should have seen when I first started out. Every time I got on the mic, I'd hear the c-word, or 'Go back to China,' all the kung flu jokes, all the small penis jokes, all the *Asian guys can't get laid* jokes."

"That's *awful,*" I say.

Teddy runs his hands through his hair. His shiny, gravity-defying, Superman hair. Teddy Yoon's got that whole Clark Kent vibe going: from the hair to the glasses to the square jaw and dorky-librarian quiet hotness.

"And it wasn't just me. Any comic that had something . . . *different* about them got heckled by the audience. And the only way to take control is to address the elephant in the room. Like, in the first ten seconds of your act. So that's what I do."

I know what you're all thinking: Who's this scrawny Asian kid, and why isn't he home studying for the SATs?

"Your race shouldn't have to be 'the elephant in the room,'" I point out.

"Brosh, it's brutal out there," Teddy says. "I know you're an *actress* and all, but . . ."

"What's that supposed to mean?"

"Because you were the cute kid on set. You probably had a million handlers sheltering you and stuff."

Right, they were really sheltering me when they would dunk me into a vat of freezing-cold green slime, take after take after take. Or the time when Nick brought a ten-foot python on set and thought it'd be funny to make just the girls wrap the snake around our shoulders. It wasn't funny; it was *terrifying.*

Teddy has *no idea.* But I just laugh it off and say, "Yeah, no."

He fidgets with his pen. The Bic twirls around his fingers. "Brosh, I know what people think when they see me." There's a hitch in his voice. "I'm not exactly . . . the six-foot-tall, blond-haired, blue-eyed quarterback."

Annie said, *Put that vibe out there!* So I say:

"Teddy, have you checked yourself out in the mirror? You're a total hottie!"

Damn. Teddy blushes. Which makes *me* blush. I can't tell if his blush is *aw shucks* or more like *get me outta here!*

The silence spreads awkwardly between us.

And Teddy talking about *his* body starts making me self-conscious about mine. We're about the same height, but he's slighter in build than I am. Under the table, I can see my thighs are bigger than his. I shift my legs so they're not smashed against my seat.

Finally he clears his throat. "Uh . . . should we try out the exercise?"

"Great idea."

We free-write for ten minutes.

Elephant in the room. List ten things people first notice about you. And not the good stuff. Teddy's comedy "advice" is kind of pessimistic. But he's been doing stand-up for two years, and I've been doing it for all of two weeks, so I give his exercise a try. Even though writing down my "traits" feels like a bad casting call: *Asian . . . Female . . . age 16* . . . not *size 0 . . .*

My name. When people first meet me, they usually comment on my name. There's that. Some people are like, *Ambrosia? That's different!* Everyone knows "different" is passive-aggressive speak for *Why the hell did your parents do that?*

Acting. People are also surprised to learn I'm an actor. They immediately feel the need to comment on your appearance: *But you look so . . . normal!*

When Teddy's hand brushes against mine, he quickly goes, "Sorry!" but then . . . he doesn't move his hand away. At least, not right away?

The mixed signals are driving me nuts.

We move on to the next exercise: brainstorming a list of pet peeves, frustrations, icks, etc. I have so many. I can't stop jotting them down in my notebook: Girls and body image. Divorced parents. Subway delays.

Teddy checks his phone. "Oh my God," he says. "I just got an audition for ROFL!"

"Wow!" I say. "Congrats!" Even though I have no idea what it is.

Teddy explains: It's a major comedy festival in upstate New York. You have to audition with a "tight five"—your funniest, sharpest five minutes of material. The audition's next Monday. "Any chance you're free?" he asks. "I could use as many people in the audience laughing at my jokes as possible. Or me, I'll take either."

"I'd love to," I say. "I'm totally free."

"Great! Thanks so much, Brosh," Teddy says. "I have to work on my LPMs—laughs per minute. The real pros can make the audience laugh every six seconds. The numbers I'm putting up are nowhere near that good."

"It's not like it's the Olympics," I say. "Don't tell me you carry around a stopwatch for that."

"What if I do?" Teddy smiles. "So I'm working on this bit about how people always confuse me with every other Asian guy they know, but the setup's way too slow," he says. "But you know what? They never confuse other white guys. So I have this joke where white girls always confuse me for Chulsoo—"

I tilt my head to a Dutch angle. "I think you look more like B-Wa, personally."

And . . . I've just about made Teddy's day. He meets my eyes, and I blush.

My phone bleeps. Liam's face blows up on my screen.

Teddy breaks eye contact. He nods at my phone on the table. "You need to get that?"

"No," I say quickly, ending the call. Why's Liam suddenly reaching out to me now? He sent one wimpy mea culpa text after ghosting me at Josie Kang's a couple weeks ago. I liked his text, just so I wouldn't seem like I was holding a grudge or whatever.

I ignore my phone. "So what made you get into stand-up, anyway?" I ask Teddy.

"Besides pissing off my dad?" Teddy shrugs. "Who else is going to call out the stupid stuff going on in the world?"

He laces his fingers around his cup. And I'm noticing how nice-looking they are, like he plays piano all day.

"You have really pretty hands, Teddy," I tell him.

"*That's* a thing to say."

"No, I mean—they're elegant," I say, backpedaling. "I mean, isn't it better than saying you have, like, hot-dog fingers or something?" I wave my fingers in the air. *"Get your Coney Island frank-fingers here!"*

Teddy stifles a laugh. "That's not bad, actually."

Liam's texting, again. I turn my phone face down. I'm so done with this.

"Isn't that the guy from *Sherlock Jr.*? As in, *the* Sherlock?" Teddy asks. I shrug, neither confirming nor denying. Teddy takes that as a yes. "Why's he keep calling you? Wait, is he the . . . ?"

Teddy lifts his arms in biceps, imitating my Liam act-out from my first mic. I stare at him in awe. "You remember that?"

"Kind of hard not to," he says. "You kept talking about your boyfriend or whatever."

"Ex," I point out. "He's probably calling about a work thing."

I'm not sure how convincing I sound, so I quickly make a joke: "Am I just some *ten thousandth follower* girl to you?"

"Touché," Teddy says, and bumps my shoulder playfully.

Chills everywhere.

We talk about the other comics; we talk about stage presence. I give Teddy some tips I learned from my years of auditions.

By the time we finish our coffees, our shoulders are touching in the corner booth. We're the only ones in the café. The chemistry between us is bubbling up in the air like crazy. We're sitting so close I can smell him: Teddy's all clean soap and spicy deodorant and coffee shop aroma.

TEDDY AND I WALK to the train together. We're idling outside the station entrance.

"Thanks for helping me with my homework," I say in my best nerd voice.

"As long as that's not the only reason we're hanging out." Teddy's voice gets all husky.

I bump his shoulder. We've been playing bumper-shoulders all afternoon. "Course not."

Suddenly I see the film montage: Teddy and me, brainstorming jokes in a café, hitting the road on a tour bus, walking down the aisle . . .

Teddy leans in. This is totally the moment: our first kiss, on the busy corner of 32nd and Broadway, as office workers and tourists getting their K-beauty fix push past us.

Except: I go in for a kiss, and Teddy's going in for a hug.

So I get a mouthful of Teddy's peppermint-spicy neck.

Awkward doesn't even *begin* to describe the moment.

"I— Ohmigod! Teddy, I'm so sorry—" I pull away fast, scooping up the dribbles of my shrinking dignity. "I thought—we were vibing, I didn't mean to assume . . ."

Embarrassment shudders through me.

"Brosh, it's cool." Teddy brushes my hair from his mouth—God, cringe—and smiles.

Then he leans in again. He tucks my hair behind my ear—*so* sexy—and draws his face close to mine. Holy shit, it really *is* happening! His lips are puckered. I tilt my face to meet his. Teddy has deep brown eyes, and lashes for days. I close my eyes and—

Teddy's lips graze my cheek.

"Bye, Brosh."

And with that, he strides off.

I trudge down to the subway tracks, more confused and mixed-signally than if we'd never "kissed" at all.

I have two missed calls and five missed texts from Liam.

Heyyy

Brosh!

Pick up!

Missed you!!

I delete Liam's number from my phone.

18

BRIDESMAIDS

INT. VERA WANG WEDDING ATELIER – NEXT DAY

An elegantly appointed Madison Avenue bridal boutique. NABI (beautiful Korean woman with a *Mona Lisa* smile, age 20? 50? It's impossible to tell, this woman must do a 12-step skin care routine) tries on wedding dresses.

She is surrounded by BRIDAL ATTENDANT (white woman, 60s), daughter CLARISSA (17yo, biracial Korean American female, tall and athletic, with the carriage of an equestrian), and BROSH (who'd rather be anywhere but here).

NABI
How do I look?

Nabi twirls, sending up clouds of ivory chiffon and lace and silk.

BRIDAL ATTENDANT
(clapping her hands)

Gorgeous, miss! Simply *gorgeous*!

CLARISSA

Beautiful, Umma! Just *beautiful*!

BROSH

You look . . . like cotton balls on steroids.

Nabi, Clarissa, and Bridal Attendant are horrified.

FLASH BACK TO:
INT. DAD'S KITCHEN – NIGHT BEFORE

DAD

Brosh, I need you to be a good sport about this.

BROSH

Doesn't Nabi have other friends she can drag to watch her try on wedding dresses? And the whole bridesmaid thing is *weird*. She didn't even give me a choice.

DAD

Nabi wants to include you as part of the family. Why is that weird?

(beat)

And don't start with the *She'll never replace my mom!* stuff, okay? Let's all be mature adults about the whole *sitch*.

Brosh smirks.

DAD
(annoyed)
What?

BROSH
(laughing)
You know what else is weird?
You trying to sound hip.

DAD
I *am* hip!

BROSH
Okay, boomer.

DAD
I'm *not* a boomer! I'm young
Gen X!

Father and daughter laugh. It is a rare moment.

Suddenly the laughter stops.

DAD
(now serious)
You're an actor, Brosh. *Act*
like you're happy to be there.
(beat)
Even if it means you have to
fake it with every bone in your
body.

RETURN TO:
INT. VERA WANG WEDDING ATELIER – DAY

The scene rewinds.

NABI
(twirling)
How do I look?

BRIDAL ATTENDANT
Gorgeous, miss! Simply *gorgeous*!

CLARISSA
Beautiful, Umma! Just *beautiful*!

The three women stare expectantly at Brosh.

BROSH
(in an Oscar-worthy performance)
I'm . . . speechless.

All the women clap and cheer.

DISSOLVE TO:
MONTAGE OF BAD BRIDESMAID DRESSES

-Saks. Brosh and Clarissa try on navy silk frocks that make them look like poor Victorian orphans.

-Bloomingdale's. Brosh and Clarissa try on yellow taffeta dresses that make them look like bananas.

-Macy's. Brosh and Clarissa try on sea-foam green satin dresses. The column-cut gown makes the most of Clarissa's statuesque figure. Brosh? Not so much.

NABI

Perfect!

Clarissa hesitates. This is the first time Clarissa's been anything but *up-beat!* all day.

CLARISSA

Really, Umma? I'm not so sure . . .

BROSH

(under her breath)

It's giving Statue of Liberty.

Despite herself, Clarissa bursts into laughter.

NABI

(not hearing)

What's so funny?

There is only one answer.

CLARISSA

Nothing.

BROSH

Nothing.

NABI

(tugging on Clarissa's snug dress)

Clarissa-ya, maybe you need to go on The Chip.

Clarissa looks hurt, angry.

BROSH

(still sotto voce)

Give me your tired, your poor . . .

Which makes Clarissa laugh again.

LATER:

Nabi goes to the cash register to pay. Brosh and Clarissa hang back.

CLOSE ON BROSH'S PHONE:

Teddy's face blows up on the screen. Then a text bubble:

Sorry can't make it to Jack's mic tonight

Break a leg

CLARISSA
(peering over Brosh's shoulder at her phone)
He reminds me of Chulsoo. Cute. If you're into dudes, I guess.

BROSH
Really? I get more B-Wa than Chulsoo.

CLARISSA
So that's your boyfriend? I see you with Neanderthal frat boys, not K-pop pretty boys.

BROSH
Okay, thanks for the non-compliment compliment.

(beat)

And Teddy's just a friend.

(beat)

Kind of. We do stand-up comedy together.

Clarissa shudders.

BROSH

What?

CLARISSA

Stand-ups are a bunch of racist, sexist incels complaining about not getting laid. Like a creepy subreddit come to life.

BROSH

Tell me how you really feel about me.

CLARISSA

Not *you*, obviously.

(beat)

Well, you are a bit of a ham. Like when you were being all dramatic or whatever at Pomegranate.

BROSH

(dramatically)

I was not being dramatic!

Clarissa gives Brosh a look.

CLARISSA

You know, for an actor, you have zero subtlety.

BROSH

Excuse you?

CLARISSA

I don't love the fact that our parents are getting married, either. Your dad's not exactly my first choice.

BROSH

(hotly)

Rude.

CLARISSA

My dad runs a Fortune 500 company. Your dad . . . trades a few crypto bonds? They're not even in the same stratosphere.

BROSH

So what are you trying to say? Your mom's like some great catch or something?

CLARISSA

Sadly my dad doesn't think so. He left her for a Brazilian supermodel.

Brosh is chastened.

BROSH

Oh.

(awkward beat)

I'm sorry, Clarissa.

(attempting a joke)

But . . . do you think the Brazilian supermodel's family's

like, *Yeah* . . . but he's no Fortune *100* CEO?

CLARISSA

That'd be a pretty messed-up cycle.

(beat)

But yeah. Totally.

BROSH

Totally.

CLARISSA

(in a more serious tone)

Ambrosia, I know you hate my mom's guts, but . . . can you just pretend like you're cool with this? My mom needs this. She's been a wreck ever since Dad left us.

Brosh shakes her head and laughs.

CLARISSA

(alarmed)

What?

BROSH

(recovering)

No, sorry. It's just . . . we have more in common than I realized. Moms-wise.

(beat)

Yes, of course. I will.

CLARISSA

Cool.

BROSH

Cool.

CLARISSA

These dresses are going to look so ridiculous on us.

BROSH

Amen, sister.

END OF SCENE.

STEPMOMS

Intro 1?

I'm getting a new stepmom. Give it up for me!

My dad and his girlfriend are "making it official."

Or as he calls it, "leveling up."*

Or Intro 2?

Everyone's leveling up these days.

Level up your job, your appearance, your life.

My dad recently leveled up.

He replaced my mom with a ~~Stepford wife~~.

~~Tiger mom.~~

~~Ivy League boss-lady?~~

Someone happy. (Come up with something better, punchier, more specific, more descriptive!)

With all disrespect to my mom*

(Pause for comedic effect. Audience won't expect that misdirection. Hopefully they'll know I don't actually mean to disrespect my own mother . . .)

My stepmom is perfect.

Ivy League MBA, beauty and brains.

She could be a targeted ad model for 12-step Korean skin care. You know, the stuff made with snail poop (Research specific examples! Deer antler extract? Tree fungus shavings?) that sells for $500 a microgram.

(Confessional tone) I have no idea how much a microgram is. Ounces all the way.

Here's the kicker.

My dad still got some other dude's leftovers!*

Her ex traded her in for a Brazilian supermodel!** (Punch line too mean? Punching down?? [But it's also true . . .])

Next thing you know, Dad will be creating a new Blacksmith family. Version 2.0!

Get your upgrade here! Get your ice-cold family upgrade here!

Okay . . . this just sounds like random free association

stream of consciousness

that's not flowing anywhere

except the toilet.

If Dad upgraded, then where's that leave Mom?

Where's that leave me?

BROSH, THIS IS NOT COMEDY!!!

Notes After Jack's Conundrum, UES:

Some jokes land; others don't. The ones with * got some laughs.

** got the biggest laughs.

Ugh, this one comic got up and spent the whole time talking about, I kid you not . . . his penis?? All the BOY comics were laughing. So dumb. His jokes weren't even funny.

(Also, he so did not use the word "penis.")

19

DAD JOKES

Dad's cooking dinner when I get home from a mic at Jack's Conundrum. The kitchen smells like dwaenjang jjigae boiling on the stove in a stone pot, and nutty barley rice from the steam cooker.

Dad did not grow up eating Korean food in the Midwest. Apparently Dad's Korean mother was forced to make meat loaf and mash every night, and it's not like H Mart existed back then. It wasn't until he met Mom that he started eating Korean food again, and she taught him how to cook. Ironically, *he's* now the better chef.

"The pupil has surpassed the sensei! *Hiyaaa!*" Dad would do a one-hand martial arts chop, and Mom would roll her eyes. "Your dad learned how to be Asian from *The Karate Kid*." We'd all giggle at the kitchen table—Dad, too.

This was when we used to be one big happy—before I started acting, and Mom and Dad started fighting all the time, and Ryan pretty much peaced out on our family.

I set the table. Something in the oven smells delicious: cheesy, gooey, and . . . spicy? It's almost like Dad's famous tater tot hot dish, but—

"Dad, are you baking with *kimchi*?" I ask in disbelief.

"Nailed it!" Dad nods, beaming. He pulls a steaming-hot casserole dish from the oven. "I call it kimchi bacon hot dish. It's one of Nabi's favorites. It's like the perfect marriage. *Ahem*," Dad adds, realizing his slipup. (My not-so-subtle clanging of the silverware might have helped.)

We sit down to eat at the kitchen island. Dad says, "I'm so glad you'll be starting at Mansfield in the fall." He means Mansfield Prep. That's what he and Mom "agreed on" for my school.

As Dad goes on about the "strong curriculum" and "university-level resources," I tune him out. Mom's still mad Dad's willing to pay for a "snooty prep school where you major in country clubs and silver spoons," but not for GDS. Even though I told Mom there was no way I was going back there. I'd drop out and get my GED, for all I cared. But Dad insisted on Mansfield Prep. Now I'm just trying to keep the peace.

As the kid of divorced parents, sometimes you go along to get along.

"So?" Dad asks. "How was shopping with Nabi today? On a scale of one to ten, just how bad was it? With one being spinach in your teeth and ten being . . . the Road to Mordor?"

Dad says it in an over-the-top British accent, like he thinks he's on *Downton Abbey*, and I burst out laughing. Not so much because it's funny—it's not, it's corny—but because Dad completely commits to the bit.

"How long have you been saving that one for, Dad?" I ask.

"All day. It came to me this morning by the Xerox machines," he says sheepishly. "Oh, right, you probably have no idea what a photocopier is. Or a fax machine, or a DVD player . . ."

I indulge him. "That's that turntable thingy with the giant cornucopia attached to it, right?"

"Good one, Brosh!" We laugh again, Dad laughing harder than me. I hope he'll forget all about Nabi, but when he asks again how bridal dress shopping went, I just say, "Fine."

"Care to elaborate?"

And talk about how each bridesmaid dress went from bad to worse? "Not really," I say, taking a bite of Dad's kimchi hot dish. It's not bad—actually, it's really good. Maybe Nabi knows what's up.

Through the rest of dinner, Dad keeps talking about the wedding. He's got it on the brain, like a groomzilla: Steak or salmon? Assigned seating separated into bride's and groom's sides, assigned seating integrated, or free-for-all? Do you think your mom will be more insulted to be invited or *not* invited?

"I don't know, Dad," I say. "Maybe ask her yourself and let her decide?"

Dad mulls this over.

This whole thing feels weird and surreal. In one sense, I

should be happy for Dad that he found "true love" or whatever. Happy that the fights with Mom have ended—where Mom would shout, Queens accent in full force, and Dad would . . . shut down, his face a blank mask. Because my father doesn't emote. And he certainly doesn't talk like a bubbly schoolgirl about cocktail napkins, and flower arrangements, and—and—and . . .

This is the happiest Dad's been in years, but I still feel low-key resentful because meanwhile Mom is sitting at home, alone. It's funny how in front of Mom, I defend Dad. But in front of Dad, I feel I always have to have Mom's back.

Teddy texts me:

I'm an idiot

I should've kissed you back

I smile down at my phone.

"Who's that?" Dad asks. "A *boy*?"

"Kind of," I say, hearting Teddy's message.

"Well, I hope he knows how lucky he is!"

"Yeah, Dad." I put my phone away. I'll think of something flirty to text Teddy later.

"Actually, Brosh, I wanted to ask you." Dad clears his throat. "Would you give a toast at our wedding?"

I don't say anything at first because I'm kind of stunned. Is it normal to ask your kid to toast you? What would I even toast Dad about? It's kind of weird because we don't usually talk much beyond:

School's out for SUMMER! I've texted Raj to come help you install the A/C. 5pm good?

Holy smokes, Batman! The news is reporting a ton of smog. I ordered you a new filter for the air purifier. It will arrive this afternoon! It's an easy install. Watch that Youtube video I just sent you.

WINTER IS COMING! LOL! I texted Raj to come help you uninstall the A/C. 5pm good? When you store it, don't forget to wrap it in a garbage bag to keep the dust out.

I won't come by, for obvious reasons.

How's your mom?

I'm still taking it all in. "But . . . why me for the toast?" I ask.

"You've always had a way with words," Dad goes on. "And your mom says you're doing stand-up now? I think it's terrific you've got a new hobby. Just don't roast your old man, ha-ha! And we're keeping it small."

I'm trying to read between the lines. "So . . . no Blacksmiths?"

Dad shakes his head. "Just us."

My father has an interesting backstory. And I mean "interesting" in the Minnesota sense, which is just a polite way of saying something sucks. Dad was born to a single mom in Korea. His mom met a man named Jeffrey Blacksmith, an American GI stationed in Seoul. They married and moved to

Minnesota when Dad was a little kid. I get the sense that Sergeant Blacksmith wasn't exactly the most benevolent of stepfathers. Apparently Dad wasn't allowed to speak Korean with his mom—"We're in America now, act like it!" So Dad eventually forgot all his Korean.

I never met my paternal grandmother. She died of stomach cancer when Dad was in high school. And I never met my paternal stepgrandfather. Sergeant Jeffrey Blacksmith is still alive, but Dad left Minnesota for college and never went back.

Read between the lines, Madame Olga used to say. *What is a person saying and not saying?* In other words, the dialogue and the vibe don't always match up. I'm Dad's only living relative who will be at his wedding. We still don't know if Ryan's coming or not. And it'd be a pretty bad look if no one from his own family said something nice on his behalf. But . . . Dad can't exactly come out and say it?

The closest he can do is crack corny jokes around it.

"Yeah, of course, Dad," I say. "I'd love to do a toast."

"Terrific, Brosh, that's terrific," he says. "Keep it short and sweet, like a miniskirt." He shakes his head. "Oof, that joke *so* did not hold up. Strike that from the record."

"Your timing was awesome, by the way," I say. "When you dropped the news about Nabi to Mom."

Dad unlaces his hands. "I didn't want to ruin your mom's weekend."

"How'd that work out for you," I ask.

Dad sighs. He doesn't love my sarcasm. "Your mom told me what happened with Stan. I know you're upset, but maybe parting ways is a blessing in disguise. Acting wasn't exactly making you happy, Brosh. It was too much stress for a kid to handle. And you've got your whole life ahead of you."

Maybe Dad's right. No more waiting for a rare job posting for your "type." No more getting your hopes up with each and every audition, when you know you're just one of a million UAFs. No more praying by the phone for a callback that you already know, deep down, will never come—all for the privilege of a one-liner that'll get cut in post-production.

At least I'll have a ton more free time. I might get straight As for once.

"It's never too late to try something new," Dad goes on. "Look at me and Nabi."

Of course he had to bring it back to his love life.

And then it's onto the groomzilla stuff: *Vanilla or chocolate cake? Jazz or new wave?*

It's hard to be happy for him when it feels like his happiness comes directly at the cost of Mom's *un*happiness.

IN MY ROOM AFTER dinner, I sit down to write a draft of a wedding toast for Dad. Toasts are supposed to be *positive! inspirational!* But I have no idea what I'm going to say about Dad that's not *Thank you for leaving us!* Last I checked, "resentful" isn't the energy you should be aiming for at a wedding. I wish Dad had tapped Ryan to give a speech instead of me.

Ryan and I were never close growing up. He got dragged along to all my acting/voice/jazz/tap/ballet/modern dance classes, headshots, auditions, and shoots, because there were two of us and only one of Mom. We barely talk now; our relationship has disintegrated to a need-to-know basis.

I text Ryan:

Hey, Dad just asked about you

Are you making it to the wedding?

I think he'd really like to see you.

Me too.

Maybe it's that he's halfway around the world, in another time zone, or he lost his phone.

But Ryan doesn't write back. He never does.

Dad's Speech, Draft #1

Dad asked me to "give him away."

It's sweet but also kinda awkward.

What was I going to say? No?

You know those mugs that say "World's Best Dad!"?

Mine would say "World's Worst Daughter!"

Dad loves band T-shirts.

His favorite is Dave Matthews Band.

They're from the 90s.

So's the T-shirt.

(Describe moth holes, musty smell, flea market vibe.)

Mom used to make fun of him for it.

"Your dad is so basic."

Dad is . . . the bee's knees.

Dad left Mom, but it's cool.

He leveled up. Good for him, bad for Mom.

Dad is . . . a dad.

(Yeah NOPE.)

Notes:

Shared a draft with Teddy. He called it . . . "tame." Said it could use some "punch-ups."

"Don't be afraid to roast him a little! Get more laughs."

Back to the old drawing board . . .

20

A NUN, A PODIATRIST, AND A KANGAROO WALK INTO A BAR . . .

Annie texts me that night:

How'd it go with comedy boy

Me:

Annie:

What the hells wrong with him

AMBROSIA LEE IS A GODDESS!!

Me:

How's Burn Off going

Are they forcing you to "cook" another PB&J

Annie:

Renegoshing my contract

But their playing hardball

FML!!

Got any good jokes

Me:

A nun, a podiatrist, and a kangaroo walk into a bar . . .

Annie:

And??

WHATS GONNA HAPPEN TO THAT KANGAROO???

Me:

idk

havent finished writing the joke

Annie:

cruel

Me:

Ugh these mics suck

No one laughs at my jokes

Annie:

well if ur telling knock knock jokes . . .

Me:

Annie:

so what gets the lols

Me:

honestly

dudes with dick jokes

Annie:

ugh

sounds like my last producer

it's like no one cares whats in ur pants

put it away

Me:

WHAT

Annie:

nm

maybe ur audience is the problem

not u

that's what my manager says

when he wants his 10% lol

what other jokes u got

Me:

Why did the husband cross the road

Annie:

y

Me:

to upgrade

Annie:

yeah

maybe don't use that in ur dads toast

ELEPHANT IN THE ROOM

The other day I had an audition.
Yup, I'm an actor. That's my day job.
That's implying the job pays.
At this point, it's more like an unpaid internship.*

I'm the least famous actor you've never heard of.
I'm like the near miss of actors.
Always a bridesmaid, never a bride!*
I'm what you'd call actor-adjacent—**
Which is a nicer way of saying a Nobody.

I'm a recovering child actor.**
You've probably never heard of me.
I'm a journeywoman, a foot soldier
deployed at a moment's notice
to end up like cannon fodder!* (Military imagery too dark??)

I'm a silent actor—
seen but not heard.
(Too self-deprecating??)

I'm a ninja actor—

operating purely behind the scenes.

Neither seen nor heard.

Sidebar: Are we still allowed to say "ninja"?*

Notes after Giggle Factory, Union Sq:

* means laughs

** means BIG laughs

People were starting to laugh at the "recovering child actor" and "unpaid internship" line. Pause and let those lines breathe.

Another day, another dick joke.

Most of the other comics left bf my set.

Wow. So not cool.

<u>DIETS</u>

What's the difference between actors and North Koreans?

(Punching down? Also: will this put me on the blacklist?)

Actors starve . . . by choice.

"No, I'll just have three ounces of bone broth! That's my quota for the day!"

(Lose the numbers? Audiences can't MATH!!)

Diet culture is our new gladiators.

Celebrities are literally killing themselves to entertain the masses. (Go into specific examples, comparing & contrasting gladiators & celebs: Jousting? Knocking your opponent off a podium? Fight to the death? "Who Wore It Better?"

I went to Melty's the other day. You know, that deli made popular by that show <u>Burn Off!</u>

I stood on line for over an hour to get a sandwich. (>1 hour? Exaggerate for comedy?)

By <u>choice.</u>

Do you have any idea how many "New York minutes" that is?

Approximately one million.

Stockbrokers everywhere were earning and losing dollars and sense. (Get meta!) See what I did there?

In the time it took me to wait for my pastrami on toasted rye with housemade mayo.

Don't get me wrong. The sandwich was >poof!<. (act-out: mind-blown gesture)

What really gets my goat (Does anyone still say this? This isn't the 1950s!)

Is the fact that I stood on line all day for the privilege

Of eating a sandwich made by an underaged chef.

Because America! (Better punch line?)

Speaking of child labor.

Child actors, amirite? (Pause after delivery. Let the punch line sit & the laughter catch up.)

You know that show *Jump! Rope! Jungle!*?

Of course you do. It's impossible not to.

You couldn't step into a Mickey D's

without being assaulted by those perky-ass, Perky Freckles toys in your Happy Meal.

They were *everywhere.*

But ever notice how all the Jump! Rope! kids on that show

Actually seem like animals trapped at the zoo?

Like puppies at the pound?

They have these sad, frozen smiles on their faces

And the try-hard, Love me, love me! vibes. (act-out: puppy dog)

What you don't know is that in actuality it was a hostage situation.

They held our teddy bears ransom

in exchange for a full day of work.

Very POW energy. (Offensive? Punching down to ACTUAL vets?)

"You won't see Mr. Fluffles again until you rehearse that double-dutch scene until it's perfect!"

Oh, you didn't know I was on the show?

Yeah, remember Golly Jee?

That's me. Season 1, three episodes, baby. (Point thumbs at self. Really ham it up!)

They booted me because I grew an ass—

which actually helped cushion the blow

when they kicked me to the curb.

They just swapped me for another Asian girl

who looked nothing like me.

But who cares, when they couldn't tell the difference anyway.

It wasn't just an ass I grew. It wasn't just boobs.

As you can see, I am not a thin girl.

I have curves, which makes me a jobless pariah in Hollywood.

(Too woe is me?? You want the audience's sympathy, not PITY!)

<u>Notes After Laughing Bobby's—Midtown East:</u>

What is UP with these other comics? They're so racist!

One guy made a Chinese joke.

Another guy made a Black joke.

Another guy made an anti-LGBTQ+ joke.

(They didn't actually use the words "Chinese," or "Black," or "LGBTQ+" . . .)

And why did all the guys in the room start to laugh??

Maybe I don't belong here.

21

CALLBACK

All week at Dad's, I work on two things: toasts and jokes. I barely hear from Mom besides some nagging check-in texts. Maybe that's also "a blessing in disguise." She won't be on my case about stand-up.

That's another problem: I keep going to these mics where there's only an audience of five or ten people, tops. And they're all just other comics who sit in the last row staring at their phones or their journals. I can't really get a good sense of how jokes land in such a small space.

The audience is infectious, like lemmings, Madame Olga used to tell us. The metaphor was awkward, but I think I know what she was getting at. The more people in a room, reacting to your material, the better you can test which jokes are funny or not.

Laughter is contagious. Even if bigger crowds are also more terrifying.

From the other comics, I learn about Atlantic Frantic, a mic that's run by lottery because it's known for getting a big crowd. I decide to toss my hat in the ring and send in a tape—as Dad always says, *You miss 100 percent of the shots you don't take!*

ON FRIDAY, I'M PACKING up my stuff to leave Dad's for Mom's. Of all the Child of Divorce problems, no one talks about the Divorced Kid Bag Schlep. As in, hauling your stuff between two households. I have duplicates of things I leave at Dad's and Mom's (underwear, phone chargers, shampoo), but I still have to pack and unpack my bag at the end of each week. Like, I'll remember to bring my favorite jeans to one house, but I'll forget the belt that goes with it at the other. Ryan's lucky he had graduated high school by the time Mom and Dad finalized their divorce.

And then I get an email: I got into Atlantic Frantic. It's happening *tonight*.

I can't believe it. I kind of sent off a tape as a joke (no pun intended). I didn't think I'd actually have to perform them *in front of a large crowd*. I wish I could talk things over with Teddy. But I've barely heard from him after his somewhat flirty last text. I don't know what's happening. Did I scare him off the last time we hung out? Is he giving me the slow fade, just like Liam? At least I'll see him on Monday, for his ROFL Festival audition.

So now I'm running around the apartment, packing my bag while rewriting jokes in my head. I'll have barely enough time to drop off my stuff at Mom's before I head to Brooklyn for Atlantic Frantic.

Dad, who's working from home at the kitchen counter, goes, "Slow down, Brosh! You're running around like a chicken with its head cut off." Even though *he's* the reason why I'm running around like a headless chicken.

Dad pulls a Tupperware from the freezer. "You forgot your kimchi hot dish!"

"Dad, no, it's too heavy," I say. I don't tell him the real reason I don't take his leftovers home. I don't want to make Mom upset. *He never made this for* us*! The nerve!* I mean, I don't know what she'd *actually* say, but no point in finding out.

Even though Dad's food is crazy cheesy, spicy deliciousness.

My phone buzzes with a 310 number. *Stan.* I figure it's a butt dial and ignore it.

But then Stan calls again. Either he really *is* that technologically inept and it's another butt dial, or I didn't sign the form his assistant forgot to send over.

I answer. "Didn't we break up?"

"Broshie, I've been trying you!" Stan says, ignoring my quip. "I have some TERRIFIC NEWS! They loved you! THIS COULD BE YOUR BIG BREAK!"

"E-Z Klean?"

"Forget the bleach! We're talking *LEVIATHAN*, Broshie! ABC!"

I'm stunned.

At first I think Stan is pulling my leg. "Are you kidding

me?" This feels like a weird, sick joke. "What happened to the whole *If the roles aren't coming to me*—"

"Yeah, yeah, I called it wrong, that's on me! Still haven't forgiven you for that STUNT you pulled. But who cares? ABC loved your SASS and REAL-GIRL ENERGY."

Dad glances up from his laptop. He can hear Stan screaming through my phone. "Everything okay, Ambrosia?"

I nod. *Stan*, I mouth.

Dad frowns. "I thought you were done with that."

Stan can hardly contain his excitement. He gushes on: The show's "expanding Claudia Chung's storyline," which means the role I auditioned for, smart-mouthed, neglected teen daughter Katie, is a "guest star" for now, but if the show's renewed for another season, which it "most *definitely* will" since it's up for another Emmy, then Katie, meaning I, could become a "recurring role." They'll all be in town on Monday—showrunner, producers, director, investors—and they want me to meet with them to talk through the role.

This is a Huge Deal.

I should be excited, too. "Hot beans!" was a silly catchphrase we'd say on *Jump! Rope!* Instead I feel . . . numb? Last month, I couldn't claw my way through a cattle call lineup for a bit part in a commercial. Now I'm a finalist for an award-winning ABC show?

Nothing makes sense.

Stan hears me not reacting. "Brosh, what's wrong?"

"Yeah . . . I'm not doing it," I say.

"WHAT?!"

"A minute ago, you said you were dropping me—"

"I didn't say *dropping*—"

"So I've closed that door. I'm done, Stan! *Not interested.*" I say it firmly, leaving no wiggle room in my delivery. "Also, I'm busy on Monday." It's Teddy's ROFL audition.

"This is ABC we're talking!" Stan argues. "THIS ISN'T THE TIME FOR JOKES."

Speaking of which.

I know it sounds crazy to turn down *Leviathan*. An opportunity like this is everything I've worked my whole life for. But I also know the feeling of waiting around for the hot guy to notice you. The guy who's so confident you'll drop everything and come running back to him, because he thinks you're lucky he chose you. I need to stop getting into these unhealthy situations.

Even if that means walking away from the likes of ABC.

Stand-up's too new to mention it to Stan right now. Because the second I tell him about it, he'll go on the same rant as Mom about sabotaging my *real* career. When stand-up is something I'm doing for myself.

"Stan, I'm kind of in a rush, so I got to go—"

"Brosh, put your mom on the phone," he interrupts.

"She's not here. I'm at my dad's. I'm actually heading out the door—"

"Then put your dad on the phone."

I do as told. "Hello, Stan . . . Yes, it certainly has been a while . . . No, no, can't complain . . ." Dad clears his throat. "Stan, I've got to respect Ambrosia's decision. No, no . . .

Frankly"—Dad's getting upset—"I don't think it's the best for her *mental health.* No. There's no need to put her on the phone again. Fine. I'll relay the message. But you know the answer. And it's *no.*"

Dad hangs up.

Whoa. I *so* did not expect that.

"Thanks, Dad," I say. "For having my back."

"You shouldn't have to thank your own father for sticking up for you," Dad says.

I pack the last of my things and get ready to go. Realize I forgot *yet another thing* and race to my room to grab a necklace. I almost trip over Dad's suitcase on the way. Dad and Nabi are leaving for LA for a week.

Dad calls out, "Brosh, did your brother mention if he was going to make it for the wedding?"

Ryan still hasn't responded to my texts. The last message he sent me was from six months ago, with his flight info so someone could pick him up from JFK.

But I white-lie, to spare Dad's feelings. "Sorry! I *totally* forgot to reach out to him. Want me to try him now?"

"No, no," Dad says. "Just, if you heard something."

Mom would always rag on Dad for being *so Midwestern.* I think she meant how he'd hem and haw and never give a straight answer. In other words, *He's so passive aggressive.*

"Okay, Dad." I hoist my bag over my shoulders. "Oh, what did Stan want to say to me at the end?"

"He said to sleep on it and give your answer in the morning."

"There's nothing to sleep on."

Dad nods. "That's basically what I said to him, too."

AFTER THE PHONE CALL with Stan, everything feels off. Like you know how in those sci-fi movies you get sucked through the vortex, and you return to your old world? Headshots, auditions, callbacks, ABC, *Leviathan*. A couple weeks ago, that was the dream—but the dream died.

So I got a new one. And now the new dream doesn't jibe with the old one. I'm thinking about all this on the train, then the bus ride home to Maspeth. Stan's call is completely messing with my headspace. And now I have to worry about what Mom is going to say when I get home, how it's going to get her hopes up for nothing. And I'll have to make peace—or try to—all over again.

But when I get home, Mom doesn't even bring up Stan's call. *I'm* the first one to mention it.

"Mom, about *Leviathan*," I start, but Mom stops me.

"There's nothing to talk about. Stan told me what you said. If you want it, fine. If you don't, also fine."

I'm not letting Mom's "coolness" go unchecked. "What's *that* supposed to mean?"

The *Leviathan* script sits there on the coffee table, like a—okay, not a tumor, but maybe like the unspoken elephant in the room.

"Brosh, I don't have time for this conversation. I'm late."

And that's when I notice Mom is all dressed up, in a silk fuchsia blouse and asymmetrically cut skirt. She *never* dresses like that.

"And where do you think you're going?" I almost add *missy*. But Mom and I haven't joked around in forever. (Ironically, not since I started stand-up.)

Mom's on her phone, not even paying attention to me.

"Out. Don't wait up."

And with that, Mom leaves the house in a cloud of her best perfume (Chanel No.19).

I HEAD TO ATLANTIC Frantic. On the subway platform, I text Annie:

Uh . . . got the callback from Leviathan

She texts:

OMG!!!! HUGE!!!!

Me:

yeah . . . gonna pass

Annie:

R U INSANE???

Me:

I'm supposed to go to Teddy's audition that day

It's kind of a big deal

Annie:

There will always be another mic

THERE WONT BE ANOTHER ABC CALLBACK

22

ATLANTIC FRANTIC

After a bus ride, two subways, and an hour and a half of my life I'll never get back, I arrive at Atlantic Frantic. I've been fine-tuning my jokes all week and am feeling pumped about my set.

But as soon as I step through the door—all my energy deflates. It's a packed house, which almost never happens at a mic, but something seems off. The air is tense—angry even. As a performer, you develop a spidey-sense for these things.

I check in with the host, this guy named Nate I've seen around at other mics. He's peacocking like he owns the place. "Teddy's chick, right?"

Since when do I "belong" to Teddy? "I have a name," I inform him.

Not that he cares what it is.

"So . . . what's with the vibe tonight?" I ask.

"A TV booker's coming," Nate explains.

Great. So now this mic is suddenly an audition. And I'm right back in a competitive waiting room.

"Oh, cool," I say. "Which TV show?"

He smirks. "Don't worry about it."

"Okay . . ." I start, but Nate's already walking away.

I'm last in the lineup. The lights dim and the first comic, Andrew, goes up.

"Make some noise if you got big dick energy!"

The room breaks into cheers and whoops.

Surprise, surprise. Another comic with another penis joke, going for the cheap laugh.

"Shut up, man." Andrew points down at someone in the front row. "You look like you're two inches, pre-shrinkage." He pinches his fingers.

The audience cracks up. But I don't laugh. I feel bad for the poor audience member getting picked on.

"I was with this chick the other day, giving her a piece of . . ."

Yeah, right. Bullshit. I swear, these guys can't imagine a world beyond what's inside their pants.

I tune Andrew out and start concentrating on my set. I page through the notes of my journal.

Suddenly I hear: "This chick's not laughing."

I look up—Andrew's jerking a thumb at me.

Oh, this hack is trying to heckle me? I don't think so.

"'Cause you're not funny!" I snap back—but Andrew talks louder over me. "She wouldn't know funny if this slapped her in the face!" He grabs his crotch.

My face grows hot. The whole room bursts out laughing. Even front-row guy, which feels like insult to injury.

"That's right!" Andrew cocks his head. "When a man talks, you shut up and listen."

The boys howl again with laughter. They shout:

"Who let this bitch out of the kitchen?"

"Watch out, you're gonna make her cry!"

I am on the verge of tears—but I'm not sad, I'm seething. And anything I say just gets drowned out by all the noise. I blink and blink and blink.

"Right?" Andrew says, nodding. "That's the problem with chicks—they can't control their emotions. So they play the fucking victim and try to cancel you!"

Boos and jeers fill the room. This isn't stand-up; it's a creepy boys' club. Right down to the *No Girls Allowed* sign.

And that's when I realize Andrew is trying to provoke me. I'm playing right into his hands. If I keep reacting, if I can't control my emotions, he'll make me an easy target for his insult comedy.

I set my lips in a straight, neutral line. I let the heat fall away from my eyes. My face goes blank, stoic. Just like Madame Olga taught us. It takes all my acting training not to give Andrew what he wants. Even though what I want is to bust him in the balls, so to speak.

And hallelujah, Madame Olga—it works. It actually works. I'm giving him nothing. Andrew gropes the air wordlessly, like a fish mouthing for a hook. He has no idea what to say next.

He moves on.

But it's too late for me. My stand-up honeymoon has officially crashed to a halt.

* * *

I DON'T PERFORM MY set. There's no point in going up and facing the firing squad, which all stuck around for the whole show, even though the TV booker was a no-show. I was a good enough actor to fend the likes of Andrew off. But I'm not a good enough comedian to get onstage and fend off revenge heckling.

The comedy world's no different from acting. Actually, it's so much worse. At least with acting, everyone's supposed to follow the script. How could I be so stupid, thinking someone like me could do stand-up?

At every show I've done, there's been at least one offensive comic who gets on the mic. I ignored it at first, treating it like *when in Rome*. As the newbie, I didn't know the culture, and if someone wanted to act like an idiot onstage, it wasn't my business.

Joke's on me. Pun very much intended.

I TEXT TEDDY ON my long trek home:

WTF is up w Atlantic Frantic

Teddy finally writes back:

Oh yeah . . . that ones not your vibe

Don't take it personally

They're just trying new stuff

Seeing what sticks

#safespace

It's too much for text. I send an audio message detailing the offensive crap that passed for jokes tonight. I tell him about the comic heckling me. I tell him the jokes were punching down.

I'm practically home when Teddy messages back:

No they're punching UP

They think girls have all the power

Me:

that makes zero sense

Teddy:

. . .

Teddy's typing dots go on for a while. Finally he writes:

Sorry brosh

Crazy family banquet

my dads yelling at me

gotta go

WHEN I GET HOME, Mom's still out. But the *Leviathan* script is exactly where we left it on the coffee table. Annie's words echo in my mind. *There will always be another mic. THERE WON'T BE ANOTHER ABC CALLBACK.*

I reach for the script and start to read.

23

KATIE CHUNG

***Leviathan* Casting Brief:**

KATIE CHUNG: Supporting, Asian Female, 13–18.

The sarcastic, smart-mouthed, neglected teen daughter of CLAUDIA CHUNG, a workaholic lawyer. The resentment is real.

The *Leviathan* script is so good, I stay up all night reading it.

I didn't think a part as rich as Katie Chung was even possible. Katie's getting into trouble at school, she acts out, all because she can't say what's really going on. She's so tired of being measured up against her perfect, big-shot Ivy Leaguer mom. Her mom, Claudia, played by *the* Sally Eum, is up for partner at the cutthroat law firm Leviathan. And Katie's dialogue is *so* snappy—all zingers and punch lines, like it was written by a comic.

The scripts I usually read for my "type" are like:

UNIDENTIFIED ASIAN GIRL: Pretty and petite, like a lotus flower. Hardworking, shy, and dutiful. Straight-A student, concert pianist and violinist, works in a sweatshop to support her family. Must know karate, kung fu, and tae kwon do. NON-SPEAKING PART.

I can't afford to blow this shot with *Leviathan*. Like Annie said: The comedy can wait. ABC callbacks cannot.

I hate being on the losing end of *told you so*.

"YOU HAD A LATE night," I say to Mom at breakfast the next morning. She got in just as I was drifting off, the manuscript still in my hands.

"Is there a question there?" Mom doesn't usually sass me, so I'm a little caught off guard.

"I read the *Leviathan* script," I say, thinking she'll take the bait. But she just stares at me like *And?*

"I meant what I said earlier, Brosh. If you say you're done, I have to respect your decision. It's your choice. I'm not going to—"

"Mom, I'm doing it," I interrupt.

She stops in her tracks. "What?"

I repeat myself, but she still stares back at me like she doesn't believe a word I say.

"You don't have to do this."

"Mom, this script is *so* good!" I say. "Why are we arguing about this?"

Something in Mom releases, like she's been holding back her excitement. "Right? *So* good! But only if you're *absolutely* sure."

"Mom. I was *born* to play Katie Chung." Which is such a clichéd thing for actors to say, but Mom laughs. "As the woman who birthed you, I one hundred percent agree."

MOM HAS SOME OF her own work to do in the morning, so we make plans to run lines in the afternoon. I've already memorized my sides, but that's just step one of acting. You have to figure out how you're going to say each line, so it "quivers with subtext and meaning" (a Madame Olgaism). You have to figure out what to do with your eyes and your body and your hands (aka "stage business"). Basically, you have to act natural so you don't sound like a robot. Even though there's a camera shoved in your face, and a hundred people on set watching you get emotional.

Mom and I get started in the afternoon. We go through the script a couple times, but something's not clicking in the fight scene between Katie and her mom.

I put down the pages. "I don't get it. Why is the mom being *so* harsh to Katie?"

"Claudia's under an incredible amount of stress at work," Mom says.

"Yeah, but still. She's kind of being a b—"

"Let's switch," Mom says.

"What?"

"Let's switch parts," Mom says. "Maybe it'll help you understand where Claudia's coming from."

"I *guess*," I say, and we switch.

And here's the funny thing: As I'm reading the mom's—Claudia Chung's—lines, I start to see things from her POV. She just got reamed out by her boss and is left to fix his mistakes, which he plays off like they're hers. She pulls yet another late night at the office, even though she promised her daughter, again, she'd be home in time for dinner.

And then I'm watching Mom, playing teenage Katie. Her voice shakes with anger, and resentment, and sadness. For a non-professional, Mom's a pretty decent actor. It's almost like she's embodying the role of Katie.

When Mom starts crying, I think, *Damn. She's going method.* Then I realize she's *crying* crying.

"Mom, what's wrong?"

"I just . . ." Mom wipes the tears on her face. "I'm reminded of . . . the day my mother died." She's groping for words.

Whoa. Mom never talks about her backstory. All I know is she was my age when her mother passed away, and that's when Mom was sent to Korea to go live with KGH.

"We . . . got into a huge fight that morning . . ." Mom starts. The day began like any other—except not. The fight was over something stupid, clothes or whatever. And Mom was being a total sarcastic smart aleck, like Katie.

Unlike Katie, Mom never got the chance to make up with her mother. When Mom came home from school, she learned her mother had been killed in a car accident.

"You just . . . never know," Mom says. "If only I'd kept my mouth shut that day! Then Umma wouldn't have been so upset, and then she wouldn't have been distracted, and then she—"

"Mom, stop," I say gently. "You can't blame yourself."

Mom shakes her head. She laughs a little to herself, like she's embarrassed.

I ask Mom what she would say if she could talk to her mother again.

She says, "I would tell Umma I'm sorry. I'm sorry, but I'm still *mad* at you. But I also love you."

Then Mom hugs me—*so* tight. And I hug her *so* tight right back.

WE RUN LINES ALL weekend. And Mom is totally right—when I return to Katie's lines, I now understand where *all* the characters are coming from. We set down our scripts, and Mom smiles at me. "See?"

"Yeah, yeah," I say, returning her smile. "You told me so."

By the end of the weekend, I feel like I've learned more about Mom than I have in years. It's like you think you know a person—but then the spotlight hits them just so, and you start to see a whole new side to them.

I tell Mom about the disastrous mic—the sexism and racism and how the guys in the room ganged up on me and I fled. And how it wasn't the first time, either.

I'm waiting for Mom to say *I told you so*. This is why she didn't want me to do stand-up.

But all she says is "Brosh, maybe you had to go through

that experience to bring this depth of character to the role of Katie."

"*Okay*, Madame Olga," I say, and then Mom does her best Madame Olga impression, exaggerated sashay and all, and I fall over laughing, and then Mom's laughing, too, and we laugh so hard we start to cry.

24

LEVIATHAN

Callbacks are a completely different animal from cattle calls. They've already vetted you. The CDs narrowed down the pool to a tiny handful, and you might could actually have a shot. In an open call, they're looking for every excuse to cut you. In a callback, they're looking for every reason to hire you. It's about your personality fit, your chemistry read with the other actor(s), and your overall vibe.

That's why I love callbacks. Just getting one feels like a win.

There's no weird psych-out in a waiting room with dozens of your doppelgängers. It's just me and Mom. She's doing her usual anxious, overly chatty thing, making metacommentary as she flips through magazines. But it doesn't irk me the way it used to.

Teddy's ROFL audition is happening right now. Last night I texted him to let him know I couldn't make it. I was *about* to spill about *Leviathan*—but something stopped me. Annie and

I tell each other about every audition. But I guess I felt like, if I told Teddy about *Leviathan*, and I *didn't* get it, then he'd start looking at me like I was a loser or something. Without realizing the callback *was* the win. And I don't need that messing with my head right now. Teddy texted back:

Teddy didn't text back. Not even a thumbs-up to acknowledge my message.

But I can't concentrate on that right now. I need to stay in the zone.

In the waiting room, I don't spend those last precious minutes before audition trying to cram my lines. I already know them cold. What I do, as I close my eyes, is try to get into Katie's headspace, just like I've been doing all weekend. I picture the scene. No—everything leading up to the scene. And not just from Katie's point of view. From the *mom's*.

Mom puts down her magazine and reaches over to squeeze my hand.

I squeeze back.

INT. CASTING ROOM – DAY

AMBROSIA stands at the center of the room. Opposite her is a casting table of DIRECTOR (white, male, mid-40s), CASTING DIRECTOR (white, female, early 40s), ASSISTANT TO CD (open ethnicity, female, mid-20s), PRODUCER 1 (white, male, mid-50s), PRODUCER 2 (white, male, late-50s), PRODUCER 3 (white, female, late-50s), and SHOWRUNNER (white, male, 40s).

CD

Ambrosia! Thanks so much for coming in today. We *loved* your tape. *Loved* it. And it's the same verve you brought to *Jump! Rope! Jungle!*

BROSH

You guys know I was only on that show for the first three episodes before they replaced me, right? I just want to make sure we're on the same page.

(beat)

To save us from a potentially super-awkward situation . . .

(confidence falters)

SHOWRUNNER

We're familiar with Jeesun Lee's work.

(off Brosh's look)

Between us, *you* had a certain sparkle. *Jump! Rope!* was never the same after you left.

BROSH

(floored)

Wow. Thank you. I'm honored. I'm *such* a fan of *Leviathan*. But you must get tired of hearing that *all the time*.

SHOWRUNNER

It never gets old.

The casting table laughs.

BROSH CONT'D

Well, if I'm being *totally* honest, I only became a fan once Claudia Chung's character was introduced. She's just so *badass*, you know? She's like the mom I wish I had. Shoot.

(cranes her neck to the door)

These doors *are* soundproof, right?

The gatekeepers laugh again. They are downright smitten with Brosh.

CD

You're a hoot and a holler! I bet you're a delight on set.

(Brosh puffs her chest with comically exaggerated confidence. At least stand-up was good for *something*.)

BROSH

I am. But you should check my references. Actors have a tendency to oversell ourselves.

Everyone laughs.

PRODUCER 1

See? Told you she has that spark.

The table murmurs enthusiastically. Brosh squints. PRODUCER 1 looks familiar to her.

FLASH BACK TO:
EXT. HOTEL EAST RIVER – NIGHT

Brosh chatting with Nick and RANDOM INDUSTRY GUY, who is PRODUCER 1.

FLASH BACK TO:

STAN

. . . Rub elbows! Network! Drum up some LEADS!!

BROSH (V.O.)

Damn you, Stan!
I hate when you're right.

RETURN TO:
INT. CASTING ROOM

BROSH
(to Producer 1)
Kang Gang! I *knew* you looked familiar.

PRODUCER 1
Guilty as charged.

CD
Shall we begin? Let's run the lines.

Enter stage left: SALLY EUM (early 50s Asian American female, willowy, beautiful). Brosh does a double take. She's doing all she can not to lose her cool and melt into a total fangirl.

Sally greets Brosh warmly. They shake hands and start to run lines from the scene. The Showrunner, CD, and Producers start whispering among themselves. Sally and Brosh stop their performance.

SALLY
Is something wrong?

BROSH
Sorry, I can totally start the scene over—

SHOWRUNNER
Don't apologize! We were just saying how nice and loose you are, Ambrosia. Most girls are so tense when they're

delivering their lines, you know? Your comedic timing is *excellent*. Carry on.

BROSH

(surprising even herself)

Okay, now you're *really* making me blush.

The casting table laughs heartily. The scene goes on. As the two actors perform their remaining scenes, the casting table is mesmerized.

FLASH FORWARD TO:

-Brosh and Sally Eum shooting on the set of *Leviathan*.

-Brosh at a fabulous Hollywood party, where for once she is the belle of the ball. The Other Jee sulks in the corner.

-Brosh at a fabulous premiere party with Teddy as her fabulous date. Liam says wistfully, "You were the one that got away!" Brosh quips, "Sorry, I leveled up."

-Brosh moves her mom into a deluxe apartment on the Upper East Side that is way bigger than her dad's condo.

-Brosh buys a mansion in the Hollywood Hills.

-Notably, there are no stand-up bits in Brosh's flash-forward fantasy montage.

BROSH (V.O.)
I've been in enough callbacks to know when I've bombed and when I've wowed. And right then and there, I knew it in my bones.
I got the role of Katie Chung.

RETURN TO:
INT. CASTING ROOM

The casting table gives Brosh a standing ovation.

BROSH (V.O.)
(in her cutesiest, *Jump! Ropeist!* voice)
Nailed it!
(beat)
I mean, for real this time!

25

GARMENT DISTRICT

Right after we leave the callback, Stan texts:

> Cart before horse but THEY LOVED YOU BROSHIE!!!
>
> Expect good news by the end of the week!

Mom and I squeal in the middle of Broadway.

"You know," she says, "it's not too late to still enroll at La-Guardia. I know your dad's set on Mansfield Park—"

"Mansfield Prep," I correct.

"Whatever," Mom says. "Even if you decide not to continue with theater—although, they *did* love you and you might be the next star of *Leviathan*—"

"Mom—"

"LaGuardia has other strong programs, and not just in theater. *And* it's a public school."

"I'll think about it." And I mean it.

WE GET GELATO TO pre-celebrate: tiramisu for Mom, mint chip for me. I ask Mom if she remembers the banquet at Caroline's house. "You don't have to answer if it makes you uncomfortable. But what did KGH say to you about Dad?"

"Who? Oh, is *that* what you call Kun-Gomo-Halmoni? That's hilarious," Mom says. "Yes, well, your great-auntie, my aunt, thinks your father left me because . . . I let myself go."

"Oh," I say. It's harsher than I thought. My mind goes to the E-Z Klean audition, where the UAFs gave Mom the side-eye. I remember *all* the waiting rooms and looks from the other stage moms. The stares on the subway. All of it.

"Mom? Can I be honest?" I don't wait for her answer. "I worry for you all the time. Because . . . I see the way people look at you. But you don't even see it."

Mom's answer surprises me. "You think I don't notice it? Believe me, Brosh. When you live in a body like mine, it becomes your superpower to shut out other people's reactions."

I let Mom's words sink in.

"Brosh, I don't know if you realize this, but your father is a very loyal person," Mom says slowly. "He would have stuck by me through sheer inertia. Because he'd feel like he'd have to follow through on his vow. But the truth is, we were both very unhappy. *I* was the one who kicked your dad out."

"Wait, what?" I say, not computing.

"Because I was lonely. And your dad was, too." Mom sighs. "We were two very different people who met when we were young, and we grew apart. We don't even have the same humor! No shade to your dad, ha-ha"—Mom, attempting slang—"but he wouldn't know irony if it hit him in the face."

"But, Mom," I argue, "You're still alone."

"*Alone* is not the same thing as *lonely*," Mom says. "You think I'm just moping at home? You don't even live with me half the time! You have no idea what I get up to."

I'm hit with way too many of Mom's truth bombs.

Mom takes a thoughtful bite of her gelato. "Once upon a time, I was . . . more outspoken. When I first got to Korea, I was sixteen, grieving my mom, and resentful. I was *so* angry at the world. I'd talk back to KGH all the time, telling her, *Lay off! You're not my mom!* I, uh, had to get that idea knocked out of me."

"Literally or metaphorically?"

"No comment," Mom says.

"Korean Auntie Trauma is real," I say.

"But it's not just individual to her. It's . . . systemic? Generational?" Mom says. "I know you're angry at me, Brosh. For not standing up for you more. For *not having a backbone*."

"That's not what I—" I stop. "Sorry about that, Mom."

Mom waves off the apology with her spoon. "But I had to learn the hard way that there's a time and place to voice your opinion. And in fact, that can be more powerful than just mouthing off all the time." Mom's honesty surprises me. "But noted. I will try to do better by you."

"Thanks, Mom." That means a lot.

I haven't told Mom yet exactly what went down during the E-Z Klean audition. I just didn't think I could stand a tirade about all the ways I wasn't measuring up. But now feels like the right time.

"Mom, at E-Z Klean, the CD said I was too big. So *that's* why I talked back," I say. "Like, you'd think, after all these years, I'd get used to the 'feedback,' aka criticism. But I haven't. So I snapped."

"What exactly did you say, Brosh?" Mom asks.

I take a deep breath. *"If I got any 'whiter and brighter,' I'd order a PSL!"*

I wince, bracing myself for her reaction. Mom puts her hand to her mouth—and starts *laughing*.

"No!"

"Yes." I nod, cringing. "It wasn't even that funny!"

Now Mom nods. "Yeah, the joke *could* use some punching up. Like, how about wearing ugly Christmas sweaters . . . No, that's played out . . . Mayonnaise and Wonder Bread sandwiches . . ."

"Ooh, consider black pepper a spice?"

Mom and I fall into a fit of giggles. People on the street stare at us like we've lost our minds, and we don't care.

"Mom," I ask, "what was the last thing KGH said to us? It sounded something like"—I butcher the Korean—"*ddok-dal-mahn*—"

Mom laughs. "똑 닮았네. It means you're exactly alike."

"You and me?"

Mom nods. "In other words: apple, tree."

I CHECK MY PHONE again, but still no word from Teddy. I hope his audition went okay. I feel guilty I wasn't there to support him. But ABC is kind of a once-in-a-lifetime opportunity. If—when?—I get the gig, I hope he'll understand.

We leave the gelato shop and continue down Broadway. We pass an old-school diner. And, swear to God, I think I see Madame Olga inside. But it doesn't make any sense. Why would Madame Olga be wearing a waitress's uniform, wiping down tables in a twenty-four-hour greasy spoon?

Has she fallen on hard times?

I grab Mom. "Is that Madame Olga?" I point to the waitress through the window. Mom peers in, then shakes her head. "I don't think so, Brosh," she says.

I look again. But the waitress is gone.

The light changes, and we cross the street.

We're walking through the Garment District. I say to Mom, "Speaking of backstories. You used to be so into fashion."

"Is there a question there?" Mom's sarcasm is thick as, well, gelato.

"Not exactly." I point to a fabric store up ahead. "It's just, have you thought about doing it again? You used to be so bold with your clothes." I remember something Stan always used to say to me. *"Why are you hiding your sparkle?"*

"Okay, Stan," Mom laughs.

We pause in front of the fabric store. "Well, out of curiosity, let's see what they've got," she says. "Since we're here and all."

So we head inside.

ANNIE TEXTS ME WHEN I get home:

So?

How'd Leviathan go?

Me:

It was

Annie:

was what?

Me:

sorry finger slipped

It was AMAZING!!!

I WAS AMAZING!!

Annie:

BROSH!!

GO GET IT!!

Me:

THX!!

Stan said they liked ok loved me

but who knows

Annie:

My agent NEVER gets feedback that quick

That's a good sign Brosh!!!

Let's celebrate

Come over tonight

Bring ur comedy boy

I text Teddy:

How'd ROFL go?

Sorry again I had to miss it

Teddy:

fine

Me:

Just fine?

Teddy doesn't text back. A half hour later, I text him again:

Hey

Hanging out with my friend Annie later

If you want to come

Teddy:

Annie as in

Perky Freckles?

Me:

Yup

Teddy:

Sure

But I kind of wonder why Teddy was so quick to respond to that and not my earlier texts.

26

ROOFTOP PARTY

Annie lives in an old sugar factory that's been converted to luxury lofts in the hippest part of Brooklyn. Typical Annie. Texting me like we're meeting up for a casual hang, and I show up to find a VIP rager with everyone wearing their sponcon best.

I pick my way through the crowd, bracing myself. I've been to this party before—standing in the corner with your phone, feeling like a total loser. But tonight's different. People I didn't even think knew I existed are now saying hi to me.

What is happening?

I keep scanning for Teddy. He's supposed to meet me here. He texted, *Almost there!* But that was a half hour ago. My battery's low, so I put my phone away. I still feel bad I had to miss Teddy's ROFL audition. When I asked how it went, he didn't want to talk about it. Which means, and maybe he's too embarrassed to admit this, that he probably bombed.

I spot my former *Jump! Rope!* cast members—Rain Bow, Jack Flash, and Double-Double—thronged together. When I saw them at the party at Hotel East River last month, they either pretended they didn't see me or ignored me. To save us all the embarrassment again, I walk right by without stopping, but Rain grabs my arm.

"Ohmigod, Ambrosia? How *are* you? It's been *forever*! You look *great*! Guys, doesn't she look great?"

Jack and Double join in the fawning:

"OMG, *so* fire!"

"I *love* your outfit!"

Which is such bullshit, because I am wearing the exact same thrifted suit and cami I wore to the last party. In showbiz, being an outfit repeater is like a crime against humanity.

Instead of calling them out on their BS, I find myself suddenly playing along:

"OMG, Rain, I *loved* you in *The Weight of Silver*! Congrats on the Oscar nom!"

"OMG, Double, you *killed* it in your Super Bowl ad!"

"OMG, Jack, *Monkey in the Middle* is my Tuesday-night must-see-TV!"

We're all doing our fake-LA voices and doing the whole fake routine of fake air kisses and fake nicey-nicey.

Rain says, "OMG, Jee is *so* jealous of you right now!"

"Why?" I say. "Because I have five followers and might catch up to her five million?"

Not my finest joke, but Rain laughs like it's the funniest thing she's heard all day. "Brosh, you're hysterical!"

"Jee hates that you're up for *Leviathan* and she isn't," says Jack.

"How do you know about *Leviathan*?" I demand.

"Word gets around, Brosh," Rain says.

"You should have seen Jee's face, she's so pissed!" says Double.

I change the subject. "So . . . do you guys still see Bobby?" I ask, referring to our sixth *Jump! Roper!*

Wrong subject. "Fuck Strawberry!" Jack says. "I hooked him up with a guest spot, but the asshole didn't even bother to show up on set!"

"Yeah, Brosh, we don't really *associate* with Bobby," Rain informs me, her voice loaded with meaning. "He went off the deep end."

Double turns to Rain. "You just said the same thing about Annie."

Rain lowers her voice to a gossipy whisper. "Difference between Annie and Bobby is one's got the cash to make her problems go away and the other doesn't. If you know what I mean."

I think Rain's waiting for me to join in on the gossip, but I'm not giving her the satisfaction. Annie was the only *Jump! Roper!* who stood by me when the rest of them didn't bother to say a word. I very obviously scan the crowd, like I'm big-timing them—a classic Hollywood move. Still no sign of Teddy.

"Ohmi*god*, it was *so* great to catch up, but I got to run," I say.

"Brosh, *soooo* great to see you!" Rain says, air-kissing me. "Let's grab a drink soon!"

"We'll watch for you on ABC!" chime in Double and Jack.

It's only once I'm away from the group that I feel I can finally breathe. It felt so claustrophobic, so dapdaphae, in that tight *Jump! Rope!* cluster. And yet, at the same time, I won't lie. It feels . . . nice to be the center of attention, for once?

So much confusion.

I feel a hand on my shoulder. Teddy? But when I turn around—

It's Liam Sweet.

"You're a sight for sore eyes, Brosh," Liam says, pressing his lips to my cheek. He's grinning his biggest, cheekiest grin. The one that says, *Yeah, that was a corny line, but I'm handsome so I can get away with it!* I'm overcome by his leather-smoky, pub-musky smell. Damnit, Brosh. Stay cool.

"Liam, you've got to stop asking ChatGPT to write your pickup lines," I say.

Liam laughs—hard. What's so messed up is that he *likes* when I tease him. I don't know if he's making nice to me because my "star power" is on the rise. Or because he knows he ranks higher than me on the food chain and I'll be grateful for his attention? But I'm so over this push-pull. What stand-up taught me, if nothing else, is that I'm no longer afraid to call out the crap.

"You know what I *haven't* missed, Liam?" I start. "How you'd love-bomb me one day and ghost me the next. God, you're such a cliché of a nineties rom-com bad boy."

"Sometimes you make zero sense but you're still adorable." Liam puts his arm around my shoulder. "Brosh—"

"Brosh?"

It's Teddy.

Liam and I break apart.

"Brosh, I got held up by the bouncer for like an hour," Teddy says. "Why weren't you answering?"

I pull my phone from my purse and find a bunch of missed calls and texts from Teddy. And I'm down to 10 percent. "I'm sorry! My battery," I say weakly. "I was looking for you, but—"

"But you were too busy," Teddy says flatly.

"Ahem," Liam says, "is this your new boyfriend?"

"No!" I say. "I mean, we're just . . ."

I blurt out no because of the kiss-confusion with Teddy last week. But now I realize my *no!* sounds like I'm trying to deny I'm anything with Teddy? I'm sputtering into hot-mess territory. I glance from Teddy to Liam, hoping they'll read my body language and get what I'm trying to put down. *It's a comedy of errors! Let's laugh at the awkwardness!* But . . . no.

"We met at a Josie Kang show," Teddy says hotly.

Liam cocks his head at me. "Same Josie Kang show I got Brosh tickets for? Glad you could fill in, mate." He slaps Teddy playfully—patronizingly?—on the arm.

You couldn't jam any more awkwardness into this scene if it were a movie. And yet—like a blur from the corner of my eye, a girl with black hair runs up to Liam and gives him a kiss smack on the mouth.

It's The Other Jee.

The mysterious bikini girl on Liam's feed. It must have been her.

I immediately right my face. I make it go neutral, scrubbing it of any trace of jealousy. Then I shoot Teddy a look like *See?*

Liam shoots me a look like *Sorry, thought you knew?*

Jee looks at me like she wants me dead. She places a possessive hand on Liam's chest. "Brosh." She doesn't do the fake-nice voice.

"Jee."

The tension is *so* thick between us.

"Uh . . . I'm gonna get a drink," Teddy says.

"Right behind you, mate." Liam drapes his arm over Teddy's shoulders like they're suddenly buddy-buddy.

"I heard you're up for *Leviathan*," Jee says. "Last I heard, you couldn't even land a soap ad."

"It was actually bleach," I correct.

"I'm surprised ABC went in a more . . . 'normal' direction."

A few weeks ago, Jee's backhanded compliment would have devastated me. A few weeks ago, I'd be tempted to return her fakery: *OMG, I'm sure they just wanted someone more down-to-earth, less diva!* But I don't. I just kind of feel bad for Jee.

"You do you," I say graciously. "Enjoy Liam. You guys deserve each other."

I find Teddy alone at the bar. "What happened to your new buddy?" I ask. "I thought it was the start of a beautiful bromance."

Teddy's not laughing. "That's that guy who keeps blowing up your phone." He narrows his eyes. "Is *that* why something suddenly came up during my ROFL audition? Too busy hanging out with the Indian James Bond?"

I can't tell Teddy about *Leviathan* because of the NDA. So I just blurt, "Liam's actually of Sri Lankan heritage."

Liam Sweet is his stage name; his agents made him change his last name from Jayasinghe so he could get more work.

I start again. "Teddy, Liam and I aren't anything. We used to be, but that's over. And we weren't hanging out last night. I, like, *like* you—"

"There you are, bitch!" Annie saunters up to us. In the span of a week, she's traded in her signature red pigtails for a new bleach-blond shag cut. Her eyes are raccoon-lined in dark kohl. Instead of a blue gingham dress and Mary Janes, she's wearing a skimpy black minidress and stilettos. She looks like a little kid playing dress-up in her mom's closet. She teeters on her heels.

"*That's* Perky Freckles?" Teddy whispers.

"You never know which version of Annie you're going to get," I say dryly.

"Brosh!" Annie says, air-kissing me. "I can't believe I'm looking at the next star of *Leviathan*!"

"Annie!" I whisper-shout. "Stop blabbing to everyone about—"

"*Leviathan*?" Teddy looks at me quizzically. "As in ABC?"

"I'm sorry, Teddy," I say. "I couldn't tell you about the callback because it's confidential. That's why I had to miss your

ROFL audition. I only told Annie because she's in the business."

"In the business," Teddy scoffs.

Annie's squinting at Teddy, like she's trying to place him—

"Ohmigod, Chulsoo?"

BROSH	**TEDDY**
This is Teddy.	We're not all the same.

Teddy shoots me a *Is she for real?* look. I shoot back, *Maybe let's give her the benefit of the doubt?* Annie shoots *both* of us a look of *Ohmigod, I just messed up, didn't I?*

"Oh my God, I'm *so* sorry! I thought you were a friend of mine," Annie gushes a mea culpa. But I can tell her apology doesn't take with Teddy. "Right, you're the stand-up guy! Got any jokes?"

"He's not going to just *perform* for you, like some monkey," I say, repeating Teddy's earlier line on me.

He doesn't go *Thanks for having my back*, like I expected. Instead he says:

"Okay, you want to hear a joke? How about this? White people are like a Benjamin Moore paint store. You have a hundred different words for white: Chantilly white, cloud white, *super* white. Yet you still can't tell *us* apart?"

Annie laughs uneasily.

"These jokes practically write themselves!" I say, attempting to break the ice.

It doesn't work.

And then Annie trips on her stilettos and spills her drink—on me.

"Oh my God! Brosh, I'm *so* sorry!" Annie tries to dab at my clothes, but she's making it worse.

"Annie, just—leave it!" I head to the bathroom and get myself cleaned up. When I get back to the party, Teddy's gone. I thread through the crowds, but there's no sign of him anywhere. I text him; he doesn't answer. Finally I catch up with Annie.

"Brosh, I'm *so* sorry!" she drawls. "I'll send you a new outfit!"

"Don't bother," I snap. "Did you see Teddy?"

"He left, maybe?" Annie shrugs.

"Did he say why?"

"Don't worry! I told him how *awesome* my best friend is and how *lucky* he is to be with you!" Annie hiccups.

My heart drops. "You said *what*?"

"Don't worry, girl! I got you! 'Member? 'Cause when you weren't sure he liked you? So I pushed him! Brosh, wanna know something? You're, like, my best friend. You're my only friend! Everyone's so fake in this fucking business. I swear to God they can all *suck my*—"

She stops herself abruptly. "If you'll excuse me, *I must attend to my guests*."

"Annie!" I call out after her, but she's already on to the next clique, the circle growing tight around her.

* * *

I LEAVE ANNIE'S PARTY. Back on street level, I can finally breathe. The rooftop party felt so stuffy and dapdaphae.

Teddy must have left because he thought we were big-timing him. I have to explain to him. To make things right.

I check my phone—it's dead.

But I think I have an idea where to find him.

27

JESTER'S PRIVILEGE, REVISITED

A half hour later, I descend the sticky basement steps to Jester's Privilege. It smells so bad: like stale beer and urine. How did I not notice the stench the first time I was here?

I stand at the back of the club. No sign of Teddy. But then the MC says, "Our next comic thinks he's the Asian Eddie Murphy! Give it up for my yellow bro from another ho—Teddy_X!"

Teddy bounds onto the stage and starts his set:

```
I recently did some charity work.

I hooked up with a girl out of
pity.
```

The crowd whoops and cheers. But I can't breathe. All the air goes out of the room.

```
I'm like chubby-girl catnip.
```

This chick, she had *the* worst dick fingers.

I'm not talking cocktail-wiener, dip-'em-in-honey-mustard, dainty little pigs-in-a-blanket.

I'm not even talking Jimmy Dean breakfast sausage.

Nope. This girl had straight-up Oscar Mayer franks for digits.

One hundred percent beef.

I'm talking jumbo-sized economy packs from Costco.

Real dirty-water, Coney Island dogs.

When a girl's dick fingers are fatter than *your* dick—

Houston, we have a problem.

"Failure to launch. I repeat, we have a failure to launch."

The sad thing is, she'd actually be hot if she tried.

But that's the problem with these "curvy" girls.

These so-called "body positivity" chicks.

They're lazy.

They mainline Oreos and wonder, "Why don't *I* look like Taylor Swift?"

Hello! It's called a treadmill. Try it sometime.

This chick, she was so desperate to get a piece of ole Teddy.

So I threw her a T-bone—

And called it community service.

Teddy brings down the house.

I should be running for the exit. But I just stand there, frozen in place. My mouth fills with a sour, bitter taste.

Humor has an aftertaste. I heard a comedian say that once in an interview. It could be the funniest joke in the world, but it still leaves a bad taste in your mouth.

Teddy's jokes are funny.

But they're also mean and angry put-downs, with a bad aftertaste.

But based on the way the room explodes, no one cares.

For once, I'm making the whole room laugh.

Too bad it's laughing *at*, not *with*.

28

PUNCH-UPS

Teddy spots me in the audience. I'm shaking with anger. We lock eyes.

He stumbles on his next line. I'm stumbling, too—pushing past chairs, feeling completely humiliated, just trying to get the hell out of there. I run up the stairs and onto street level.

"Why are you here, Brosh?" I hear Teddy's voice behind me. He must have left his set and followed after me. We're standing face to face.

"What the *hell* is your problem, Teddy?" I say. "How dare you stand up there and make those jokes about me? They were mean, and offensive, and—"

"Why do you think those jokes were about you?" Teddy's face is an unreadable mask. "I know you're still new to stand-up, but facts don't get laughs. It's comedy, not CNN."

"Tell yourself that all you want," I say. "I told you the body stuff in confidence. Also, you stole my hot dog joke!"

"Oh, please. That hot dog fingers joke is from *Everything Everywhere All at Once*."

I didn't even see it, but whatever.

"I thought you were better than all those other comics," I say. "Instead, you just punched down at me!"

"Punched down? I was punching *up*!" Teddy says. "Brosh, you were the one calling all the shots, going to parties with your celebrity friends, while I was just *some guy* to you."

"I liked you, Teddy. I *trusted* you," I say.

"*Liked* me? Please." Teddy spits out the words. "You know what I realized at Annie's party? You only invited me because you feel sorry for yourself. You're one of those girls who just feeds off the attention of guys you can get to make yourself feel better about the guys you *can't* get. Like Liam."

"That's not true—" I argue.

But I stop myself. *Is* it true? Did I make Teddy feel lesser-than? And was I only with guys like Liam for the status—like a Hollywood stamp of approval? If I'm being honest, that might be how it started out, yeah. I was in a low place, and Teddy literally sat in for Liam at Josie Kang's show. But my feelings for Teddy are—*were?*—genuine. We had an instant attraction and connection. There's no faking that.

Teddy looks down at his hands. It's a tic I've noticed he does when he's anxious.

"Brosh . . ." His voice trembles. "I'm *not* some consolation prize."

I own up. "I'm so sorry I made you feel that way, Teddy," I

say. "The truth is, I'm insecure about a lot of stuff. I'm trying to work on it, but . . ." I trail off.

I start again. "Teddy, I'm so sorry I hurt you," I repeat. "I really wish you told me how you were feeling so we could have talked about it."

"When? Over mani-pedis?" Teddy tosses out the words like they're sharp, sarcastic knives.

I explode. "What the hell are you talking about? I practically *threw* myself at you, Teddy! You were the one who pushed me away. Because I'm not, like, skinny or hot enough for you?"

Teddy doesn't say anything. For once, he's at a loss for words.

"You know what *I* realized, Teddy?" I say. "It's not that girls like me are too 'curvy.' It's that guys like you force *us* to be smaller so you can feel bigger and better about yourselves!"

Just like high school, just like Hollywood, and, apparently, just like stand-up.

"So this is your MO. Anyone who gets the slightest bit on your bad side, you retaliate by ripping into them onstage and in public? Is *that* how you got your ten thousand followers or whatever?"

"That's not what I meant!" Teddy says.

I add an extra jab. "And by the way, pro tip: You muffle your delivery. You could *really* use an acting class."

Teddy gropes for words. "I bombed my audition today, okay? It was awful, Brosh. And I just—I needed a new tape. So I started riffing and the guys started laughing, and . . . I just went with it." He stares down again at his hands.

"You and I have *very* different ideas of what's funny."

Teddy's eyes meet mine. "It wasn't supposed to be like this," he says defensively.

We just stare each other down.

"Goodbye, Teddy," I say, and walk off—trying to put as much distance between him and me as possible.

29

PIED-À-TERRE

I'm on the elevator up to Dad's apartment. All I want to do is curl up on the couch like a little kid and forget all about Teddy. Dad and Nabi have already left for LA, so I'm guaranteed to be alone.

But when I get to his place, I hear talking on the other side of the door. I let myself in—

It's Clarissa. We both jump.

"What are you—"

"What are *you*—"

"I thought you'd be at your mom's," Clarissa says. "Umma said I could stay here while they're in LA."

"Doesn't your mom have her own place?" I ask.

"She put it on the market," Clarissa says.

"I'm . . . gonna go?" says the face on the other end of Clarissa's phone.

"Who's *that*?" I ask after she ends her call.

"Just some girl." Clarissa tosses her phone aside. "So what's with you?" she asks.

I'm realizing now how I must look like to her: all dressed up in my going-out clothes, with splotchy red eyes to match. (I kind of cried on the subway ride home.)

"Just some guy," I say, trying to laugh it off.

"It's *always* about some girl or guy." Clarissa pats the seat next to her on the couch. I slump down next to her. "Want to talk about it?"

"Not really."

"Me neither." Clarissa nods in the direction of her phone.

"Cool."

"Cool."

The silence spreads awkwardly between us. And because I'm me, I suddenly find myself filling it.

"I was, like, at my friend Annie's party tonight. And I invited this guy, Teddy, and things got . . . weird."

Bit by bit, I start telling Clarissa about what went down. I can't believe I'm actually opening up to her. But she's acting nice and . . . sisterly? And it feels good to get this load off my chest.

Clarissa strokes her chin like she thinks she's Freud. "As your unnie—"

"Here we go." I roll my eyes comically.

"What Teddy did was *so* not cool," Clarissa says. "But . . . I also kind of feel for the guy? He was probably so intimidated being at that party. You're, like, famous."

"I'm not!" I argue. "I'm a has-been, at best."

"You can drop the false modesty," Clarissa says. "Before we met, my mom was telling me all about you: how awesome and accomplished you are, in that typical Korean mom way that just made *me* feel like a total loser." She chuckles. "Brosh, I was so intimidated to meet you."

I'm stunned by what Clarissa's saying. Nabi's always been chilly, at best, with me. And Clarissa was a total snob when we first met. I guess I had it wrong.

Also: Clarissa's never called me Brosh before. It feels familial.

I say, "You're the one who's Ms. Perfect Prep School and Future Ivy Leaguer—"

Clarissa snorts. It's the least "ladylike" thing I've seen her do. "Stop. I'm like the biggest goof on campus. I'm in an improv troupe at Choate. But there's only so much 'yes, and!' you can do with trust-fund boys from Connecticut. They're *so* fragile," she says. "Also, I'm only applying to Columbia to make Umma happy. That's like the *last* place I want to go."

Once again, Clarissa and I have more in common, momswise, than I thought.

Clarissa's eyes fall on the TV console. "Wow, your dad still has a DVD player?"

"He got it in the divorce," I say. I chuckle to myself, remembering Dad and my corny joke about obsolete technology. The DVD player is ancient. Honestly, I don't think I've ever seen it being used. "Want to give it a whirl?"

"Sure, why not?"

We riffle through the drawer of DVDs and find Josie Kang's first comedy special. I had no idea my parents owned it.

"Have you ever watched this?" I ask Clarissa. "It's a classic."

Clarissa shakes her head. "I only know *of* Josie Kang because other comedians always mention her. We never really watched stand-up at home. My mom's more into *America's Funniest Home Videos*."

"Oh my God, that's like Dad's favorite show!" I say. "Mom hated it. They used to fight about how corny versus funny it is."

"Anyway," Clarissa says, nodding at the DVD. "I'm game if you are."

"Should I get the popcorn?"

"No popcorn," Clarissa says. "I checked."

And then I remember Dad's leftovers in the freezer. I pop the Tupperware into the microwave.

"Clarissa, you *have* to try this kimchi hot dish my dad made."

She sniffs the air. "Smells good. Your dad cooks? My mom can't cook to save her life."

I laugh. "Neither can mine."

"Your dad really knows how to pick 'em."

We grab the hot dish and two forks and hit play.

30

ROAST

The next night, at Mom's, I have a dream about Dad and Nabi's wedding. Actually, it's a straight-up nightmare.

The reception is held in a giant white tiled bathroom, like the E-Z Klean Bleach set. Nabi is not Nabi at all, but Sally Eum, my *Leviathan* mom. I keep trying to escape the wedding, clawing at the white tiled walls, but there's no door, no windows, nothing. We're all trapped.

All I can smell is bleach.

Suddenly, the setting changes: It's not a catering hall; it's the set of *Jump! Rope!* And Mom and Nabi are sitting at a table together, ignoring each other, both wearing white. And now it's my turn to give Dad's toast.

"I'm so honored to get to speak at Dad's wedding," I start. "Because this will be the most face time I get with him since he divorced my mom!"

I start clapping—like really doubling down. Reluctant applause breaks out. Because people are lemmings. They'll do anything you order them to do.

"This 'toast,' or should I say 'roast,' has been in the books for a long time. Dad's secretary had to pencil me in. She goes, 'Hon, he's got an opening on Saturday, eight to eight-oh-five p.m. I could squeeze you in.' Because when you're the child of divorce, you take whatever slot you can get!"

"Ambrosia!" Dad calls out from the sweetheart table. *Ambrosia.* Not *Brosh.* "That's enough, ha-ha!" His tone is light and fake, like fat-free butter popcorn.

I ignore him and spew forth *all* the one-liners:

"Dad ghosted Mom, and he's not even white!

"The ink's not even dry on their divorce papers, and dearly beloved, here we are!"

I let Dad have it—vomiting out everything I've wanted to say for the past two years. The whole cast of *Jump! Rope!*, including The Other Jee, is there. They're all laughing without me. Teddy is there, too. He's cracking up. Clarissa scowls at me from the audience.

I lift my champagne glass. "Anyway, congrats to Timothy Evan Blacksmith! Let's toast wedding number two!" Then, in an exaggerated sotto voce: "In case this doesn't work out, Dad, I'm also available for weddings three, four, and five!"

Silence. Not even a clap.

The MC rushes to grab the mic from me. "And . . . let's give it up for the daughter of the groom!" His laughter is over-the-top, like he's trying to bring back the positive vibes in the room. It sort of works. Over the audience's laughter, the MC whispers to me, "Word of advice, kid? Read the room."

I feel a rush of sick bubbling up. I run away from the reception hall/*Jump! Rope!*/E-Z Klean set. I collide with Clarissa.

"You're a disgrace!" she screams.

"Runs in the family!" I scream back.

I launch myself at the toilet and vomit.

And then I wake up.

With the worst aftertaste in my mouth.

31

HOLLYWOOD-READY

I sleep like crap, tossing and turning for the rest of the night. It's dawn before I finally drift off again. Next thing I know, Mom's standing over my bed, shaking me awake.

"Brosh, it's Stan!" Mom says. "It's about *Leviathan*!"

Something in my gut tells me it's not good news.

But Stan's face is big and smiley on Mom's phone. "Brosh! They LOVED you!" he gushes. "They think you've got acting chops for days! The word *PRECOCIOUS* might have been thrown around. Ditto *PRETERNATURAL TALENT*."

"Ohmigod. Ohmigod!!" Mom and I are screaming, jumping around the house. I'm a little too old for superlatives like *precocious*, but I'll take it.

I need this win so badly. Especially after what went down with Teddy and my short-lived "comedy career." It would be the ultimately *F you*.

"And everyone who met with you, all the producing partners, you knocked their socks off, Broshie!" Stan goes on. "You stood out above your competition. They loved your real-girl energy. And they *especially* loved your SASS."

My brain is ignoring the backhanded compliment of "real-girl energy," which kind of sounds like industry-speak for *unattractive.*

Mom is thanking Stan, the usual obsequious *OMG, you work so hard on our behalf* spiel she always gives whenever he calls with crumbs.

But this isn't crumbs. This is the Real Deal.

"Next is the screen test!" Stan says.

Mom squeals into the phone. My heart, literally, skips a beat. This is *huge.* The screen test is like the last formality before you get the green light. You actually have to negotiate your deal and sign your contract right before the screen test.

Everything I've worked so hard for—all the rejections, the humiliations, everything—is it all finally coming together? It feels too good to be true.

Stan goes on about the deal, and how he's going to negotiate hard: an escalation clause with each episode, plus extra for the opportunity costs of signing a non-compete. In short: It'll be more money and fame than I've seen in my whole life. *No-man's-land,* my ass.

"There's just one thing."

I stop jumping around. My heart stops again—for different reasons. There's always a *just one thing.*

"What is it, Stan?" Mom asks cautiously.

"The camera LOVES you, Broshie. No doubt. And you

have beautiful bone structure, thanks to your mom and dad. It's just . . . buried."

"Buried." I have echolalia.

"Yes. You're a little soft. We just want to . . . to sharpen you up. To present your BEST SELF on camera."

I'm too shocked to speak. He goes on. "They just want you to drop down a size, maybe two. NO BIG DEAL. We'll get you a trainer. Maybe even get you a doctor, see about getting you a little boost to help you along. They're willing to take this chance on you, Broshie! We can't afford to squander this. And by the time you come in for the screen test, you'll be SLIMMED DOWN and HOLLYWOOD-READY."

"Is that what you're saying, or is that what *they're* saying?" I ask.

"Broshie, it's just the way it is," Stan says gently. "Plenty of actresses drop the weight. You're a pro, Broshie, you got this! You worked too hard for too long to throw it all away. Not for an opportunity *this big*. Not when you are THIS CLOSE."

That's all I have to do. Just lose the weight. Obsess over every calorie again and exercise until my body wants to drop. I did it once before. I can do it again.

The sad thing is, she'd actually be hot if she tried.

At Annie's party, it felt good when everyone fawned around me instead of brushing past me like I was invisible. But it also felt fake at the same time. Like eating fat-free chocolate bars—you get the sugary rush, but the mouthfeel's all off.

"Broshie?" Stan pauses. "Brosh? Broshie? Are you still there?" Stan calls out again.

"Ambrosia, Cindy, they're sending over preliminary paperwork today. Are we good to move forward?"

I look at Mom. She looks at me.

ME		**MOM**
`Yes.`		`No.`
	`(beat)`	
`What?`		`What?`

We stare at each other in disbelief.

Stan stares at *us* in disbelief.

I said yes. Because after the week I've been through, I want to be *seen*. Because the Teddy_Xs of the world pretend to want to hang out with me but make jokes about me behind my back. Because the Liam Sweets would be fine skulking around with me behind the scenes but would sooner be seen in public with The Other Jee than with me. And I'm so sick and tired of it all.

"Stan," Mom says, "my daughter is already Hollywood-ready. They can take Brosh as is."

What is happening? My mom, sticking up for me? She doesn't even send back the wrong order at restaurants.

"*As is?* Cindy, this isn't a real estate fixer-upper," Stan says. "THIS IS IT. Chances like this won't come again. Especially not for Brosh's type. We should take it."

Stan addresses me. "Brosh, you're for this! Right? Maybe you're scared it's going to be too much hard work? We can fix that. Science is a WONDROUS thing, what with all the shots and—"

"Stan, stop!" Mom interrupts. "You've made us act so grateful to you for these opportunities that come our way. But what were the opportunities you were making for *us*? Stan, for years you've been doing the bare minimum for my daughter. You were looking for any and every excuse to drop her. Sorry, Brosh, I know that's hard to hear."

I cannot believe Mom is actually saying these words aloud.

Stan's eyes go from Mom to me. "Broshie, this is YOUR career. YOU call the shots. And you've been in this biz for long enough to know how rare an opportunity this is. Remember pilot season? That was the last time you had any real heat on you. After *Leviathan*, your phone will be ringing off the hook."

Just ten more pounds.

But after that, will it be *another* "just ten more pounds"? And another?

Will they take and take and take, subtracting away from me until I'm at zero?

"Stan, do you believe in me?" I ask.

"What kind of question is that? Of course I believe in you, Broshie. Don't be ridiculous," Stan says.

"Do you believe in me enough to 'sell' me *as is* to *Leviathan*?"

Stan says nothing.

"You told me they loved my *real-girl energy*," I say. "Why is it such a crusade to get a straight-sized girl on camera? It shouldn't have to be just stick or cow. Especially when you see how many 'diverse' male bodies get screen time. Every time I turn on the TV, it's just a bunch of dad bods!"

"You're asking the impossible of me," Stan says quietly.

"Then . . . I think we're done here," I say. "Goodbye, Stan."

I'm shaking all over after we end the call; I slump to the floor.

When I steady my breath, I say, "Remember when Stan mentioned pilot season two years ago? Mom, I was . . . starving myself. I wanted it so badly, I was willing to be unhealthy to get it . . ."

Mom looks disturbed, distraught. "When you were in LA?"

I nod. "You were back home, dealing with all that stuff with Dad, and Ryan, and you'd already sacrificed so much for my career, and I couldn't tell you because I felt like *I* had to be the strong one—"

And suddenly the tears are streaming down my face. I swear I'm not crying on cue, even though it's a "Special Skill" listed on my résumé (along with tap, jazz, and juggling). I can't stop the big, fat, messy tears splashing everywhere.

Mom holds me as I sob into her chest and spill. "I needed you, Mom!" I am ugly-crying.

Mom's ugly-crying, too. "I'm *so* sorry, Brosh! I'm *so* sorry I wasn't there for you . . ."

She wraps her arms around me tighter, fiercer—like she's trying to protect me from the outside world.

"This business, it feels like—like I'll never be good enough," I say. "And I think that's why I connected with the role of Katie, because her mom keeps pushing her to be perfect, when she so isn't, and . . ." I trail off.

"I can't believe I never saw the signs, Brosh," Mom says. "A mother's job is to protect her child. And . . . I was so intent on making sure you felt safe *on* set, that I wasn't as focused on everything happening *off* set. I'm ashamed you felt like you couldn't come to me with this."

"You had a lot going on," I say between hiccups. "In your defense."

"That's no excuse," Mom says. "Are you okay? Should we make an appoint—"

"Mom, I'm fine. Really," I interrupt. "It was a long time ago. And we can talk about it later. Promise."

Mom takes a deep breath. "Brosh, ever since you were a child, you had a natural confidence. When the doors kept *opening* for you, when every CD or director you met with was so taken with you . . ." Mom says. "I can't even tell you, as a mother, how proud that made me feel."

It's a little strange to hear Mom say this, because I always felt *weird* walking into those auditions. Like, all these adults were too try-hard in front of me, like they wanted something from me. As a kid, you can smell the BS from a mile away.

Any confidence I had walking into the room was because I'd prepared for the roles.

And I realize that didn't all come from me; it came from *Mom*.

"But I only felt confident because you helped me prepare for the roles," I say to Mom. "Not just running lines, but you'd help me figure out the character's backstory. Like . . . what's her favorite color or ice cream flavor, but also what are her hopes and fears? Mom, I couldn't have done it without you."

It's the truth.

"Thank you for saying that, Brosh," Mom says, touched. "I was watching this interview with Josie Kang on Instagram. She talked about how few opportunities she had as an Asian American female in Hollywood."

"True," I say just as I'm thinking, *My mom's on* Instagram*?* She barely knows how to order a pizza online.

"Apparently she finally got her shot, but it was a crappy deal," Mom goes on. "One part of her brain said, 'Be grateful! Take the deal!' But the other part refused to compromise. So Josie Kang stood her ground. She knew her worth, and she got what she wanted. No—what she *deserved*. That woman is *fire*."

"So fire," I say, even though everyone stopped saying *fire*, like, yesterday. "Wait. Since when do you follow Josie Kang?"

"Please. I've been Kang Gang for longer than you've been alive," Mom says. "And I had all her old specials, but I lost the damn DVD player to your dad in the divorce."

I wrinkle my nose. "You weren't missing much. The old stuff doesn't age well, anyway."

Mom nods. "Yeah, I prefer her later work. It's more emotionally honest."

"Is that what made you stand up to Stan just now? No offense, but it was kind of out of character."

"Maybe I'm taking a page from your book." Mom squeezes my hand. "I'm dropping the mic."

ACT III

DRAMEDY

I'm the one that I want.

—Margaret Cho

32

HOTEL EAST RIVER

The following headline blows up in my feed: *From BURN OFF! to BURNOUT! Where Did America's Sweetheart Go Wrong?*

Accompanied by a photo of Annie with raccoon eyes wearing a skimpy black outfit, tripping and flashing her bits to the cameras.

The same outfit she was wearing at her rooftop party earlier this week.

I immediately text Annie:

Are you ok

She writes:

Annie:

Im soooo fucked

Me:

Are you back in NY

I'll come over

Annie:

Don't!

Too many paps

I'll drop a pin

Annie's camping out at the Hotel East River. I head there after school, bearing candy.

"Room service," I say, holding up a package of Sour Patch Kids. Annie's favorite.

She eyeballs me through the peephole. "What's the secret password?"

"Hot beans," I answer, and she lets me in.

Annie stands in tattered pajamas. Her hair, unbrushed and unwashed, hangs limply, brown roots starting to show. Her face is bare and makeup-free.

"I forgot your freckles are wash-off-able," I say.

"Har-har."

I follow Annie inside her hotel room. I'm trying to contain my envy as she leads me through her enormous suite. The balcony overlooks Central Park. The dining table is covered in gift baskets and bouquets of flowers. But a trail of candy wrappers and ice cream containers litters the floor, like some deranged sugar monster went on a rampage.

"What are you doing cooped up in here?" I point to the balcony. "I'd be out there all day if I were you."

"Can't," Annie says. "Paps have long-range lenses."

Annie flops onto her bed. Her bright blue eyes are bloodshot.

"My career is over, Brosh," she says. "Kaput. Donezo. DOA."

"Do you know how the photos got leaked?"

"Mom thinks it's a smear campaign. Who knows," she says flatly. "It could've been anyone."

"Can't your publicist spin this?" I ask. "Girl becomes woman, sows her wild oats, yada yada. *Girls just wanna have fun!*"

"Girls don't *get* to sow their oats," Annie hisses. "Brosh, I have a 'nice girl' image to uphold." She lowers her voice. "I wasn't even drunk! Well, barely. I just tripped on my *stupid* heels, and some dirty pap snapped the money shot. Meanwhile, no one cares if Jee's out partying because that's her 'brand.'"

"I'd argue that *this* is the real money shot." I pinch my fingers into a viewfinder.

"If you're trying to make me feel better, it's working," Annie says, laughing despite herself. "My lawyers are saying *Burn Off!* might sue me for breach of contract. It was two seconds of my life, and now my whole career is *ruined*."

"But people love you, Annie," I say. "I'm sure it'll all blow over."

"I'm running out of cash, Brosh," Annie says. "I need this job. I can't just start over and go get a job flipping burgers."

She sits up in bed. "Remember when you asked me why I

don't just walk away? I wish I *could*. I know you don't believe me," she says. "But I'd give it all up in a heartbeat to have my freedom. If only I didn't have this face everyone recognizes. It's, like, not even mine anymore."

I knew some of Annie's troubles over the years, but this is the first time she's opening up to me, so naked and honest like this.

"Brosh, don't take this the wrong way. But you have no idea how lucky you are. You had the choice to walk away and try something new. I wish *I* could just . . . drop the mic on all these assholes and say what's *really* on my mind."

"It wasn't exactly a choice—" I interrupt.

Annie holds up her hand—*let me finish*. "And I know you're, like, whatever about your family, but you had a good support system, you know? Your mom . . . she was really great. Cindy always looked out for you on set. And she looked out for me, too. Some days, I wished I could go home to *your* mom and not mine," she says. "That's a big deal Cindy stuck up for you about *Leviathan*." I texted Annie the news that I took myself out of the running. "My mom would've been like, *How much? Tell me where to sign!* When you've got a deadbeat dad, an addict for a mom, a greedy-ass stepdad, and four siblings all counting on *you* as their meal ticket . . ." Annie laughs bitterly. "You have no choice but to play the part."

This whole time, I kept thinking how *Annie* was the lucky one. She's offered more roles than most people—me—would see in a lifetime. But she's stuck with a label she never asked for.

I fold my friend into a hug. "I'm so sorry, Annie."

It's not fair Annie has so much on her plate. People think

it's so cool to be famous. But they have absolutely no idea what the cost of that fame is.

"Thanks, Brosh. Sorry to trauma-dump on you. But you're the only person I can really talk to."

Annie offers her signature dimpled smile, but I can see the tears welling up.

I put on my best gossipy voice. "Well, *I* heard that Taylor and Kim are beefing again," I say. "Hate to break it to you, Perkins, but by tomorrow you'll be yesterday's news. Literally."

My joke works; Annie manages a laugh. "I don't know what's worse." She takes off her sunglasses and wipes her eyes. "Bad publicity or obscurity."

"Definitely obscurity." I point my thumbs at myself. "I can't even get a table at Starbucks."

Annie laughs again. "So? What's going on with your comedy? When am I going to get to see you tell some jokes?"

"Nope. I'm retired," I say. "Stand-up's a young man's game."

"You barely started!"

"After all that went down with Teddy, I don't know . . ." I shrug.

When I told Annie about Teddy's roast the day after, she swore he would be her mortal enemy.

"Forget that clown!" she cries. "Forget *all* those sexist clowns! Why should they decide whether you do stand-up or not? If you give up now, that's like letting them win. I've seen the clips you sent me, you're *good*, Brosh."

I tell Annie I'll think about it, even though my mind's already made up.

* * *

ANNIE SEES ME TO the door. "I'm sorry you have to deal with all this," I say. "It's not fair."

"Eh, I'm sure my team'll come up with something." She spreads her arms, like the matter's already out of her hands. "They *better.* I'm paying them a fortune."

We hug goodbye.

"Maybe one day we'll all laugh about this," Annie says. "Isn't there that saying?"

I finish her thought. "'Tragedy plus time equals comedy.'"

33

HOW TO STAND UP

Mom's been on my case about stand-up, too. She tells me about an online intro stand-up class she found. "It's only for a month, and it won't interfere with school," she says. "Maybe try it and see."

I'm confused. "But you said stand-up was stupid."

"First off, I never said it was *stupid*," Mom corrects me. "I had *reservations*."

"Reservations are for restaurants. You straight-up vetoed it," I say. "Anyway, I'm done. It's so hard to go to these mics and make people laugh. The audience, and the other comics, they're so toxic." My voice got small. "Mom, I don't even know what's funny anymore."

Mom says, "*I'll* be your open mic. We'll run lines together."

"Stand-up doesn't work like that. They're jokes, not scenes."

"Why not? I've always found the most compelling stand-up comedians tell stories," Mom says. "I know you think acting and stand-up are worlds apart. Boys like that Teddy might fire off artillery rounds of *joke-joke-joke-joke*." Mom mimics a machine gun. "But *you* know how to harness a full range of emotions: anger, joy, grief, passion. And most importantly, empathy. You can bring all of that to your comedy." She looks me in the eyes. "Brosh, *acting* is your superpower."

I GO INTO THE class half-heartedly. Joke's on me, because so far, so great. We learn the actual structure of a joke: setup, punch line. That's it. It's a loose formula that applies to all styles of comedy, from one-liners to observational bits to personal stories. And then there's experimental comedy, which plays with that form.

I kind of wish I'd taken this class *before* I first started going onstage. It would have been so helpful to understand all the basics first, instead of trying to DIY stand-up. I once asked Teddy if he took a class, and he just looked at me like I was nuts.

"None of the guys take classes," he scoffed. "Why should we, when there's YouTube and open mics?"

Suit yourself, I think now. Because in class, we get meaningful feedback from both our instructor and other students. And I'm not just learning from one person; I'm learning from all twelve of us.

OUR INSTRUCTOR, LARA, IS a sassy older comic with giant glasses that take up most of her face, and a helmet of shockingly black hair, despite her wrinkles. On the first day of class, she told us, "The guys I started out with make blockbuster films and date models; I teach an online stand-up class to beginners." She looks familiar, but I can't place her. Maybe she has just one of those faces?

Teddy used to obsess over LPMs—laughs per minute—but Lara tells us it's a poor metric for true comedy. "LPMs are bullshit," she says, in her no-BS delivery. "Do you want to go for the cheap laugh? Be my guest. But I'll take quality over quantity any day."

For homework, Lara makes us watch our favorite comedy sets on slo-mo and transcribe the bits, line by line, by hand.

"This feels like a waste of time. Isn't that what AI is for?" someone asks in the chat.

"Technology won't teach you the pacing of a joke," Lara says. "This is *human* work. Nothing to it but to do it."

It does feel like a waste of time. But when I sit down and do my homework, and I stare down at the page, I realize: The bits are like a *poem*. The line breaks are like stanzas. There's repetition and rhythm and metaphor. I'm reminded of Sheng Wang's avocado joke, and I see it all starting to make sense.

All those times I zoned out in Shakespeare class ("Mў/ mís/ trĕss'/ éyes/ ăre/ nó/thĭng/ líke/ thĕ/ sún!"), I could have actually been learning something about stand-up.

Touché.

I do what I always do when preparing for a role: I study comedy like it's the frigging SATs. I'm not a good student at school stuff, but I totally nerd out when it comes to craft.

For our own jokes, Lara makes us write and rewrite them.

She takes a red pen to our pages and slashes through them (okay, it's Microsoft Track Changes, but same difference). I write and rewrite, like a hamster panting on the wheel.

I have way more respect for writers than I used to. This stuff is *hard*.

AT THE END OF our class, we'll have "graduation": We'll perform a live, in-person set. Which means I have one month to write, rewrite, memorize, and perform my "tight five"—a polished, five-minute set chock-full of my best jokes.

Mom becomes a stage mom all over again: Except now she's my comedy buddy. I practice lines over and over, with different wording and intonations.

It's one thing to kick ass from the safety—shelter, cocoon, womb—of your home, performing for your mom.

It's a whole other thing to be performing it at *the* Gotham Laugh Cellar—where Josie Kang famously got her start.

No pressure.

34

CORNY CAT MEMES

I'm over at Dad's, and he has a whole process for pour-overs. Mom buys pre-ground beans from Costco, and she programs the coffee maker the night before. She needs her morning jolt first thing, but Dad doesn't mind waiting twelve fussy minutes to do the whole ritual with the bottle-nosed kettle, and the cone filter, and the temperature monitoring. I'm not really *supposed* to drink coffee, but on weekends, Dad lets me have one cup.

Dad's got the TV on hockey, playing highlights from last night's game. Dad's a hockey nut, and the Wild might still stand a chance for the Stanley Cup playoffs.

"I hear you and Clarissa have been bonding," Dad says, setting the kettle to exactly two hundred degrees Fahrenheit—a soft and steady roil, not a boil. "Nabi was telling me. We're really glad you girls are getting to know each other better."

I nod. "She's cool."

Clarissa and I exchanged numbers after our sleepover at

Dad's. She returned to school after spring break, but we said we'd hang out again before our parents' wedding next month.

"And how was meeting Nabi's family?" I ask Dad. Nabi's sister lives in LA, so he met some of his soon-to-be in-laws on their trip there.

"Well, they were all on my case for not speaking Korean," he says, and wags his finger: "*A Korean should know how to speak their language.* Nabi's making me do Duolingo, but it doesn't take. The ole noggin's full." Dad taps his head.

"Mom used to make fun of your accent when you tried to speak Korean," I say. "She said you sounded like a Yank."

"I remember your mom's bullying well," Dad says, laughing.

The coffee is ready. He pours two cups.

Dad says he and Nabi have decided to rethink the whole concept for the wedding. "Since this is the second marriage for both of us, we've decided to be more . . . casual about it."

"But what about Nabi's *Vera Wang custom gown*?" I press my hands to my face in mock horror, like the mask from the *Scream* franchise.

"I'm going to ignore that," Dad says. "Actually, Brosh, Nabi said you girls don't have to wear matching bridesmaid dresses. You can wear whatever you want. *Tasteful*, of course. Don't show up wearing jeans or anything."

"That's . . . actually pretty cool of her," I say.

"Nabi's cooler than you give her credit for," Dad says.

We're standing on opposite ends of the kitchen island. "So, Dad," I start. "I'm trying to work on your wedding toast. But

I'm honestly drawing a blank. I'm kind of still . . . processing my feelings about you getting remarried."

I don't tell Dad about my dream—nightmare—of roasting him at his wedding. But it dredged up some really real emotions that still stay with me.

Dad says, "You're entitled to your feelings, Ambrosia. Just as your brother shared his with me, too. And if we're being honest, I don't like . . . this." He indicates the distance between us. "Ever since your mom and I got divorced, it's like you're giving me the silent treatment. I know you're upset, but I'm still your father. I deserve—"

"Deserve *what*?" I surprise myself, my voice rising with emotion. "You didn't fight for us. Forget me—you didn't fight for *Mom*. I know she said *she* was the one to kick you out, but it kind of feels like you checked out the second she 'let herself go.' The ink's barely dry on the divorce papers, and now you've just moved on?"

"A lot more goes into a marriage than you realize." Dad sighs, cradling his cup.

"I don't understand, Dad," I say, normalizing my voice. Or trying to. "I thought . . . you guys were happy."

"We were, for a time." Dad's pet peeve is lukewarm coffee. He's always microwaving his mug every five minutes so it'll keep to temp. But he just lets his coffee grow cold.

"It's kind of a long story. Do you really want to get into all of it?"

"I do."

Dad gets up and puts his cooled coffee in the microwave. I guess the conversation can't be put off any longer. We're still standing across from each other at the island, so Dad gestures us over to the couch and switches off the hockey.

It's not that I haven't heard Mom and Dad's meet-cute. I've just gotten different fragments over the years. But this feels like the first time I'm really getting to hear it from his side of things. They met at a bar in the West Village—Down the Hatch or one of those—when they were both in college (Mom: Parsons, Dad: NYU).

"Your mom was this total punk rock girl from Queens," Dad says. "She comes up to me and says, 'You look fresh off the bus from Kansas.' I couldn't tell she was joking, so I blurted out, 'Minnesota, actually.'"

"*That* was Mom's opening line?" I say, laughing.

Dad laughs, too. "Right?" he says. "But what's funny is that your mom was the first person in my life to peg me as a Midwesterner. My whole life, people just called me 'Oriental.'"

In Dad's small town in Minnesota, he was the only Asian kid for miles. His Blacksmith name never matched his face. His mom did everything to appease his stepdad, which meant giving up Korean culture at home. Most days, Dad didn't even know *how* to be Asian.

"I never felt like I belonged, not even in my own family," Dad says. "Until I met your mom."

Mom was the first to introduce him to K-Town—not just the 32nd Street one, but the OG Flushing one. She took him to family banquets and gave him a taste of home: all of his forgotten favorite childhood foods. For the first time in his life, Dad felt like he finally belonged.

I already know Mom's side of the story: "Oh, please! Your dad only picked me because I was the first Korean girl he laid eyes on."

"Your mom and I couldn't have been further apart," Dad goes on. "She wore Doc Martens, went to art shows, and rocked out to the Ramones. I wore chinos, majored in accounting, and listened to Dave Matthews Band. But that was part of the magic between us. At least, at first."

I'm surprised to hear Dad confiding all of this to me about his marriage.

"Until you got divorced," I say. "When Mom had to be with me in LA for pilot season. My acting always got in the way."

I'm overcome with emotion, thinking about that time. I still haven't told Dad about my ED. I know it sounds kind of double-standardy that I only told Mom. But I'll tell Dad when I'm ready. Soon.

"That's *when* it happened; that's not the *why*. Brosh, sweetie, it had nothing to do with you. Things with your mom had been a long time coming." Dad stops to warm up his coffee again. "When you've been together with someone so young . . . Brosh, we were babies. Barely older than you are now. Neither of us were fully formed. Your mom and I, we're *very* different people."

Dad laces his fingers together, then unlaces them. He does that when he's anxious.

Teddy used to fidget, too. Weird.

"Even when we had Ryan, we were starting to grow apart, if I'm being honest. And that distance grew over the years. It wasn't any one thing. Get to my age, Brosh. And maybe someday you'll understand."

I think about Teddy and me. Even though I'm so angry with him and he hurt me, I still miss him. It makes no sense, but feelings are feelings.

"It doesn't mean I don't still miss your mom," Dad says. "She was a real New Yorker: sarcastic and hilarious. Every party we'd go to, she'd make people laugh."

I never really stopped to think about it: Mom being funny? I guess I never thought of her as much beyond just *Mom*. But then I remember all of her little sarcastic quips.

Maybe that's Mom's superpower.

"Yeah, unlike you, with your corny dad jokes. Which I *so* hope isn't hereditary," I say. "I guess we'll find out when I roast you at your wedding!"

Dad laughs. "You are your mother's daughter."

I realize Dad's right. Apple, tree.

"Your mother made me into the man I am today. And I will always, *always* be grateful to her for that. I don't know if you know this, Brosh, but it's not easy being an Asian man in America. You know how Hollywood works. At best, we're typecast as the dorky, FOBy butt of the joke. If I never saw *Sixteen Candles* again, it would only be too soon."

I saw *Sixteen Candles* on streaming the other day. Clarissa mentioned she was writing a paper on it for an Asian Studies class, so I decided to put it on. It was painful watching Long Duk Dong, the "Oriental" exchange student, deliver each of his cringey, caricaturized lines to Molly Ringwald. Actor to actor, I knew Gedde Watanabe, who, by the way, was born in *Utah*, had no choice but to follow the script.

I think about Teddy's comedy. How he'd get heckled with all the racist Asian-guy jokes.

Dad studies my face. "How's your fella? The one you were doing comedy with?"

I answer tentatively. "He wasn't who I thought he was," I say. "In fact, he was kind of a jerk."

"Want to talk about it?"

"Not today."

"Fair enough." Dad nods. "What I will say is that boys your age are very insecure. They'll do anything to follow the herd."

"But *you're* not like that," I say.

"You don't know what I was like in high school," Dad counters. "Look, I don't know what happened between you two. But sometimes, when people act in hurtful ways, it's not about you. It's because they never learned to love themselves." He pauses. "Brosh, in this world, there are two kinds of insecure people: those who beat themselves up and those who beat up others."

His words sink in. "Damn, Dad. That was *deep*."

"Can't take the credit. I heard it on a podcast yesterday," Dad admits sheepishly.

When we finish our coffees, I ask, "Dad? How did you know when it was finally over with Mom?"

He says, "It's when the thought of staying hurt more than the thought of leaving."

"And how do you know when you've found the right person?"

"When . . . it feels like you and the other person complete each other. Like, you're on the same page and you laugh at all the same jokes. And your mother and I—we just kind of stopped laughing altogether."

Mom's a sarcastic New Yorker, and Dad's an aw-shucksy Minnesotan. They don't even like the same comedians. Dad finds Josie Kang crass; Mom loves her. And I'm . . . somewhere in between.

Did Teddy and I ever laugh at the same stuff? We didn't even agree on Josie Kang's funniest jokes. He prefers her older, "edgier" stuff, which I find kind of dated and offensive. I like her newer, more personal stuff, which Teddy finds kind of boring and tame.

Then I think about everyone close to me in my life: Annie and I laugh at the same dumb stuff. Liam and I bonded over Josie Kang, but any time he attempts a joke, it's all corny and try-hard. Mom and I laughed more in the past couple weeks than in as many years.

"Dad. I don't want you to be a stranger. I don't like . . . *this*." I repeat his earlier gesture, indicating the space between us. "I need you to show up for me. And not just, I don't know, sweep things under the rug and act like everything's okey dokey. Which I know is, like, impossible for a Minnesotan . . ."

"A daughter shouldn't *have* to hold her dad accountable."

Dad squeezes my hand. "But it was also a wake-up call. I haven't been there for you. And I need to be."

Dad folds me into a hug. And I hug him back.

The door opens; Nabi is home from spin. "Hey, Brosh!" she says brightly. *Brosh?* I file it away under *That's new*. Dad hands Nabi a pour-over.

"Tim, you *have* to watch this. So funny!"

Nabi holds up her phone. It's that corny-ass cat video that's making the rounds. Mom showed it to me, too, with a disclaimer: "I feel like my IQ just dropped twenty points."

Nabi starts up the video, and she and Dad, no joke, start laughing their heads off.

"Play it again!" Dad says, and they're hunched over her phone, wiping the tears running down their faces. He's looking at Nabi, his eyes filled with tenderness and . . . love? And Nabi is giving Dad that same look back.

I've never seen Dad give that look to Mom. Or maybe he did, way before my time. Maybe even before Ryan's time. And I also realize: Mom never looked at Dad like that, either.

Seeing Dad and Nabi laughing together, looking so comfortable and cozy with each other—maybe humor is a kind of home.

35

QUEENS COMEDY

It takes all my courage to get back onstage. I'm talking serious wound-licking, nervous-sweating *God, I am so dreading this*-ing. Not that I have a choice if I don't want to fall on my face at my graduation show in one month. So I figure my performance will be like the first pancake, which always sucks, and check out this mic in Queens that my instructor recommended.

I text Annie again on my way to the train.

Hey checking in again. You ok?

I haven't heard from her since I saw her two weeks ago. At least the headlines have moved on to something else: A Marvel superhero trolled a C-lister in his last movie, and it's all the celebrity gossipers can talk about. Annie, as predicted, is yesterday's news.

She texts just as I'm about to walk up to 7 Train Mic.

Annie:

Yeah

That blew over lol

And she sends me a link to an article in *The LA Times*: *America's Sweetheart Donates* Burn Off! *Profits to Children's Hospital Los Angeles!* Accompanied by a photo of Annie, dressed as Perky, surrounded by little kids in hospital gowns.

I write:

is that a flex?

Annie:

Only cost a small fortune

Me:

The life you lead

Annie:

the life u left behind

hey want to come to my premiere next fri

I'll put u on the list!

Me:

Can't wait to COOK OFF OR BURN OFF!!!

Annie:

Me:

Send me the deets

Can't wait

Jumping into a mic

Annie:

YEAH BROSH!!

Get back out there!!

Has-Beens

I'm an actor. Give it up for me!*

You may have seen Spider-Man, Dune, Only Murders in the Building . . . *

Oh, I wasn't actually cast in any of those.** (Misdirection!)

But I auditioned for all of them. They said, "You did great, kid! Don't call us, we'll call you!"***

That's Hollywood for never in a million years.***

Yes means maybe, and maybe means no.

Nobody actually says no to your face.

I only found out I didn't get my last role

when I saw Zendaya's face on the side of a bus.** (Play dumb. Really commit to the delivery to get the lols.)

It was for Quantum Echo Hunters.

(Tag) I guess she screen-tested better in green.** (Even bigger LOLs. Hallelujah to the humiliating Jump! Rope! party for giving me that joke.)

If my career's a dating app, my ass has gotten swiped left on more times than most people go number two.**

Notes After 7 Train Mic:

Found a new mic in Queens. Wow, vibe is WAYYY cooler.

People actually told FUNNY jokes without having to be crass.

It feels less . . . punching-downy, you know?

Maybe Alt Comedy is more my scene?

Can't wait to go again next week.

36

BURN OFF! KIDZ EDITION

On Friday, Mom helps me get ready for Annie's TV premiere. She brought out a bunch of her old dresses and let me have my pick. A gorgeous emerald-green one caught my eye, and Mom tailored it to fit me. It looks custom-made.

"You know you can come, too," I say. Annie texted me: *Bring Cindy!!*

Mom's on her knees with a mouthful of pins. "No thanks. Not my scene. There," she says. "This drapes *beautifully*. You're stunning, Brosh."

We stare at my reflection in the mirror. The dress *is* stunning. And, in my totally biased opinion . . . *I'm* stunning in it.

"Look at you, having your *Pretty in Pink* moment!" Mom says. "Except Molly Ringwald's prom dress was fugly as hell."

For once, I get Mom's '80s reference. "It wasn't *that* bad," I say.

Mom makes a final adjustment to the hem of the dress and gets off her knees. "Oh, you girls are going to have so much fun! Tell Annie congrats, truly. I can't believe you're all grown up."

"Thanks for letting me wear your dress, Mom," I say. "*I* can't believe I get to wear a Cindy Lee original."

"I couldn't have asked for a better model."

MY CAB PULLS UP in front of the Natural History Museum. The line for Annie's premiere of *Burn Off! Kidz Edition* goes around the block. That's the line for the "civilians"; Annie put me on the guest list with a plus-one. When I invited Clarissa, who apparently is the biggest "Burnee," she wrote:

Judge Kelly is my SHERO!!!!!

Mom loves Host Dennis

He is ajumma catnip

Must be the Dad joke energy

Me:

so is that a yes

Clarissa:

FEEL THE BURN!!!

Clarissa's coming from a meetup with her improv team. She'll probably be the only person in a cocktail dress practicing, "Yes, and . . . !"

She arrives in the cab behind mine. She emerges in a cloud

of sky-blue taffeta, like Cinderella. "You look amazing!" I say, giving my sister-to-be the biggest hug.

"No, you!" she says. "That green is *gorgeous*."

I pull Clarissa to the VIP entrance. "C'mon, we're on the list."

And even though I usually roll my eyes at the jerks who get to cut the line and get waved past the velvet rope—

For once it's nice to have friends in high places.

INSIDE, ANNIE AND THE other stars pose for all the flashbulbs on the red carpet, in front of the *Burn Off! Kidz Edition* marquee. Annie is camera-perfect in a cornflower-blue gingham dress, white bobby socks, and black patent leather Mary Jane shoes. Her hair's dyed to its *Jump! Rope! Jungle!* strawberry, and her pigtails jut from the sides of her head like bicycle handlebars. She is all bright smiles and freckles.

Which I know is a total front because she was forced to sign on to another season of the show.

Clarissa is straight-up starstruck. "Ohmigod, it's Judge Kelly!" and "There's Chef Jackie!" She keeps pointing to this and that person, like she's a kid at Disney World. I shrug; I'm no Burnee. And this is just another work event. But I sometimes forget that for civilians like Clarissa, it's a big deal to see TV people in the wild.

"I still can't believe this is your world," Clarissa says, then grips my arm. "Wait, is that Host Dennis? Umma will kill me if I don't get a picture with him. How gauche would it be to ask for a selfie?"

I flutter my eyelashes at her fancy word. "How *gauche*? Very." I give her shoulder a gentle nudge. "Go for it." Clarissa runs over to Host Dennis with her phone. He gives her a toothy, bleachy grin and mugs for the camera.

Annie comes over to say hi, momentarily released from the red carpet. "Thanks for coming, Brosh. It means a lot you're here." She massages her cheeks, presumably sore from nonstop smiling. "Just one more night of this dog-and-pony show, then I can finally let my hair down."

"If they ever let you retire those pigtails," I say. "I'm sorry you had to re-sign for another season."

"Oh, don't pity me, Brosh. I drive a Porsche. I have a house in the Hills, a loft in Brooklyn, the house in Tulsa—"

"And, and, and." We laugh.

"Hey, I'm coming to your show at Gotham," Annie says. Then, off my confused look—"Cindy sent me the info."

I shake my head. Once a stage mom, always a stage mom.

"Or . . . don't?" I say. "My jokes kind of suck."

"Let us be the judge of that."

Annie's eyes fall to Clarissa, getting a selfie with Host Dennis. "Hey, who's *that*?"

"That's my *sister*, Perkins."

"Not yet she isn't." Annie winks and strides off.

THE AFTER-PARTY IS IN full swing. At the bar, I bump into The Other Jee—or she bumps into me.

"So I don't know if you heard," Jee says. "But I just got a callback for *Leviathan.* I figured it's down to you and me."

"Congrats, Jee," I say. I actually mean it. "They didn't think I was the right 'look,' so I'm out. But I really hope you get it."

I don't put on my best LA voice, I don't give her some face-saving, image-preserving excuse. I just tell her the truth.

I'm waiting for Jee's smug, judgy reply. But—she doesn't.

"I hate how our whole career, you and I have been competing for the same handful of roles," Jee says. "Every role I lost, you won."

Her honesty catches me off guard. "Same," I admit. "Honestly, I was so jealous of you."

"And I was so jealous of *you,*" Jee says. "Before *Jump! Rope!*, you got *all* the 'cute Asian girl' roles! I mean, there were, like, barely any. But still." She lets out a bitter laugh. "Every time I came home from another failed audition, my mom would yell at me: *Why can't you be more like Ambrosia? Why don't you make the CDs like you more?* So Korean mom."

"*So* Korean mom," I say. Even though Mom, to her credit, never compared me to Jeesun Lee.

"My biggest career break was getting your leftovers," Jee says. "And now it's even harder. It's tough out there, Brosh."

I hazard a guess. "*Jade Opium*? Or *Lair*, or *Motel*, or whatever it's called?" Jee nods. "Yeah, I think I was offered *your* leftovers."

Jee shrugs. "Just another Tuesday in the business."

"Ugh," I say. "I hate that there's not enough work to go around."

"*Jump! Rope!* wasn't all that it was cracked up to be," Jee says. "In fact, you dodged a bullet by not staying on."

"What do you mean?"

Jee's face darkens. "It . . . wasn't the best time."

She doesn't say more.

Jee finishes her drink and sets the empty glass on the bar. "You know what's funny? In a different world, you and I might have been friends."

I nod, agreeing. "You're probably right. I hope you get it, Jeesun," I say. "*Leviathan*, that is." I actually mean it. I hold up a fist. "Fighting."

Jee returns the gesture. "You'll find your spotlight. You always do. The camera loves you, Ambrosia Lee."

AT THE AFTER-PARTY, AS Clarissa fills her phone with a million selfies, I catch Annie again on the red carpet. She's still posing for the last of the cameras, flashing her thousand-watt smile, setting off her world-famous dimples, forcing her best face for the cameras.

The paps can't tell, and neither can the fans at home. But I know it's just an act.

You're free, Brosh.

Maybe someday Annie will be, too.

37

TOAST

Two weeks later, Dad and Nabi tie the knot at a tasteful converted warehouse/gallery/event space in Dumbo. It's actually less of the extravagant fanfare than I thought it would be. Clarissa said her mom's initial invitation list of five hundred (!!) had been whittled down to fifty guests. Still, I'm getting jittery thinking about giving my speech later in front of all these people.

I do the deep breathing exercises Madame Olga taught us. Four seconds in, hold for seven, out for eight. I got this.

I think.

Dad decided the right thing to do would be to invite Mom. And Mom sent a gift card with a nice note in the mail but declined the invitation.

It's nice when your parents act like grown-ups.

After the ceremony and the cocktail hour, the wedding reception speeches begin. Honestly, they're dry as toast. Work friends praise Dad's "hardworkingness" and Nabi's "determination," like keywords on a résumé. I swear they were written by AI. Besides one memorable speech by Nabi's friend Jane, where she shared a story about how Nabi was such a huge fan of *Friends* that she gave herself the English name Rachel, the rest are as anemic as hospital Jell-O.

Clarissa gives a sweet if overwrought toast filled with watery metaphors about her mom being "unmoored" before she found her "harbor" in Dad as they "embark on this ship called life." I'll tease her about it later—*What is this,* Moby Dick*?* But I see Nabi tear up and decide I'll hold my tongue.

And then it's my turn. The mic goes *hsss!* when I adjust the stand to my height. Everyone winces until the screeching stops.

"I'm Ambrosia, daughter of the groom. I'm so honored to get to speak at my dad's wedding. You know what they say: Second time's a charm!"

I laugh, to signal to the audience it's okay to make a joke. They laugh. Because people are lemmings. They'll do anything you order them to do.

"To be honest, when Dad asked me to give a toast at his wedding, I was like, 'Uh, Dad. Are you sure this is a good idea? I'll have a live mic. You want a toast or a roast?'"

I'm following Teddy's advice: I'm addressing the elephant in the room. But what Teddy got wrong is that it's not always about the physical "weakness." By addressing the *emotional* elephant head-on—*Uh, this girl's dad's marrying someone who'll replace her mom? Awkward!*—I'm releasing the tension in the room and again giving the crowd permission to laugh.

And they laugh—hard.

Dad calls out from the table, "That's enough, Brosh." Just like he did in the dream.

But I don't stop. I keep going:

"For anyone who knows Dad, you know how passionate he is about three things: jam bands from the nineties, ratty T-shirts of jam bands from the nineties, and corny jokes. My whole life, that's what I remember most. When you look up the definition of *dad joke* in Merriam-Webster, there's a picture of Timothy Evan Blacksmith."

The audience groans at the corniness of the joke. That was the point.

"In case you missed it, I just made a dad joke *about* a dad joke."

A couple of *really* robust laughs.

"One of Dad's all-time hits is 'I love seafood! When I *see food*, I eat it!' Wocka-wocka."

The crowd goes wild.

I tag the joke: "And to add insult to injury, Dad laughs at his own jokes, like he's his own TV laugh track."

The laughter keeps rolling. I wait for it to die down before pivoting to my next bit.

"My father's an accountant. We all have our vocation. Doctors are out there, saving people's lives. Firefighters are out there, saving people's lives. Dad's also out there, saving people's . . . taxes, one income bracket at a time. Hey, we're all doing our part!

"But his *true* calling is rescuing Dave Matthews Band shirts from the bin at Goodwill."

Nabi laughs, giving Dad a fake pinch on the arm. So far, so good.

"But I recently learned something new about Dad. Something I never knew before. My father was like . . . Dorothy from *The Wizard of Oz*."

People laugh, even though that's not part of the joke.

"And not just because they're both from the Midwest. Dad, like Dorothy, was trying to find his way back home. And for most of his life, Dad never felt *at* home.

"For those of you who don't know, I used to be an actor. In my line of work, you have to play make-believe. You have to sell fantasy as authenticity. On sets, I had a fake house with a fake mom and a fake dad, white picket fence and all. And the only way I could 'sell it' was by closing my eyes and pretending I was at home in our little house in Maspeth. Which, by the way, is actually surrounded by a chain-link fence, because we keep it classy in Queens.

"It was lonely on set. But I knew, at the end of each day, I could go home, to my *real* home, and not be lonely anymore.

"To be honest, I wasn't exactly jumping for joy when I learned Dad was getting remarried. In fact, I took the news pretty hard. And not just because I watched *Cinderella* too many times—seriously, that's a straight-up horror flick; it should *not* be rated G! For one, it perpetuates evil-stepmother stereotypes. Two, it violates labor laws. Three . . ." I stop ticking the list off my fingers. "I could go on, but I'll spare you.

"I took Dad's news hard because I thought I was going to lose my sense of home.

"The difference between Dad and me is that I got to take 'home' for granted. I always knew home was 58-34 Newtown Avenue, Maspeth, New York 11378. Dad, unlike me, did not have that privilege.

"Nabi, everyone's already praised your brains *and* beauty; I'm left speechless. Folks, you could have saved me some material! Seriously, if you choose to quit the whole Fortune 500 boss-lady thing and become a lifestyle influencer or whatever, sign me up. I'll be the first of your millions of followers.

"But as your new stepdaughter, I want to say, from the bottom of my heart: Thank you. Thank you for being 'home' for Dad. Thank you for taking away his loneliness, his home*less*-ness, and replacing it with happiness. And a lifetime of corny cat memes."

Nabi laughs.

"And as your new stepdaughter, I have one, selfish plea: Please *never* stop making Dad feel at home. Because . . . he's my dad, and I love him."

I blink away tears; I can't help it. I sense sniffles in the crowd. I can't end my speech on that note. So I finish with a callback:

"Nabi, I hope you were serious about the 'in sickness and in health' stuff. Because Dad's T-shirts of bands from the nineties also haven't been *washed* since the nineties. And you've got a roomful of witnesses."

That brings down the "house," pun intended.

I'm trembling—from the rush, and the adrenaline, and the sheer emotion of it all. Whether or not I got the laughs, it wasn't the point. I spoke from the heart. We all raise a glass and toast the happy couple.

When I make my way to the family table, Dad is wiping the tears from his eyes.

"Brosh," he whispers, "how did you know all that about me?" He squeezes my hand—tight—like he's holding on for dear life. I realize I am Dad's only family here.

"I know all your tells, Dad." I squeeze his hand back. "I've been studying you my whole life."

I could have chosen the roast. I could have humiliated Dad and gotten more laughs, more likes, more buzz.

Instead, I chose grace.

RYAN ARRIVES LATE TO the wedding, just as Dad and Nabi do their first dance. None of us knew if he was actually going to come. "What'd I miss?" he says, reaching for a slice of vanilla buttercream cake.

"Just my *awesome* speech," I joke.

"That was on purpose."

Ryan's so dry, I can never tell if he's joking or not.

Even though he's the older sibling, Mom always used to tell me I needed to be protective of Ryan because of all the attention I got being a child actor. So I'm kind of perpetually walking on eggshells around him. We've never been close.

"Did you know Dad was never a Korean citizen?" he asks suddenly.

I forgot about Ryan's famous non sequiturs.

"But Dad was born in Korea," I say. "Dad came to the US with his mom when he was around five or six. So he should have birthright citizenship, right?"

"Nope. Kids had to be registered under their dad's name. And Dad had no dad," Ryan says.

"But what about his mom—" I start to ask, but I already answer my own question. Dad was raised by a single, unwed mother. Which means Dad was a child without a country.

"Why else do you think our grandma married some random American soldier and peaced out of the country?" Ryan says. "Apparently the law's changed now, too late for Dad."

"That's . . . not cool," I say. I'm kind of caught flat-footed, because I was so not expecting to be having this conversation with my brother about our dad, at his second wedding of all places.

"Yeah. I just found that out when I popped over to Korea from Koh Samui."

"Oh."

"God, look at them," Ryan says, nodding at Dad and Nabi, dancing.

"Well, they *did* just get married."

"Mom and Dad were never like that," Ryan says. "And I should know. I'm their love child."

"Okayyy . . ."

"You couldn't find two people more different. I shouldn't even exist." Then, after a pregnant pause: "And technically, neither should Dad."

I have no idea how to respond to that. Maybe if Ryan and I were closer—but that's never been our vibe.

"No one knew if you were coming," I say instead.

He shrugs. "Mom convinced me to. Said it was my 'filial duty' or some shit." He swallows the last of his cake. "I'm gonna say hi to Dad, then bounce. See you."

Ryan tosses his fork down and gets up from the table before I can say goodbye.

THE NIGHT WINDS DOWN. I head to the bathroom. Someone's leaving as I'm going in. She looks *so* familiar. Is that—

"Oh my God!" I breathe out. "You're—"

"Yeah, yeah, yeah," she interrupts. "Let's spare both of us the embarrassment."

It is JOSIE KANG.

"Sorry, I don't usually fangirl . . ." There are so many things I want to say to Josie Kang:

Thank you for being my comedy hero!

How did you make it out of this biz alive?

CAN I FORCE YOU TO WATCH MY TAPES UNTIL YOU GIVE ME FEEDBACK???

All I manage is "Why are *you* here?" Which . . . just sounds like the rudest thing ever.

How did I not see *the* Josie Kang at the wedding until now? If I'd known she was going to be here, I would have punched up my set, hammed it up with more jokes . . .

"I'm related to Nabi, don't ask how. They put me in the

cheap seats." Josie Kang holds up her phone. "Look, my Uber's coming in a minute, and that's how long I got until I explode from my Spanx. But you were real good up there. Funny, and you got heart. And I don't just say that."

"Wait! Uh . . . thank you! Do you have any advice for me?"

Josie glances at her phone. And I realize I'm being kind of rude. The poor woman was just trying to pee before heading home.

"I'm sorry, I'm holding you up—"

"The second I stopped trying to be part of the boys' club, that's when I spoke my truth," she says. "It's a long road. Keep at it, Ambrosia Lee."

And with that—Josie Kang disappears into the night.

38

FINAL ACT

It's a packed house at Gotham Laugh Cellar. I should be all nervous jitters, but I'm actually not. What's the worst that can happen? I totally bomb, no one laughs at my jokes, I forget all my lines, the room fills with dead silence, and as I exit the stage, I slip on a banana peel, ensuring my public humiliation forever and ever, amen?

Big whoop. I've had worse.

I'm wearing my yellow dress, which Mom helped me style. She was the one who actually suggested I wear it. "What happened to *it's a little loud*?" I ask.

"Tonight's your night, Brosh." Mom smiles. *"Get loud."*

DURING MIC CHECK, I meet the other members of our online class: lawyers, bankers, college students, even a retired firefighter—it runs the whole gamut. Everyone seems nice and super supportive. Our instructor, Lara, couldn't make it, which is a bummer.

I've gone a couple times now to the 7 Train Mic. And wow. The energy was way cooler and more supportive. The comics actually told funny jokes, without having to be offensive. And there was not a single dick joke—which feels like a low bar to have to hurdle, but sadly *isn't*.

The alt-comedy scene is, well, much more my scene.

It's a friends-and-fam crowd, and I can already feel the warmer vibe. My whole party is here, sitting at my reserved table: Mom, Dad and Nabi, Clarissa, and Annie. Clarissa said she was bringing a friend from school. Annie and Mom pick right up like old times. But when I see Mom and Dad only greet each other with a curt nod, my chest tightens. Will there be beef? But . . . hopefully they'll all be adults here, right?

Since Dad's wedding last weekend, I've written and rewritten my set. I took the jokes I've been working on during spring break and scrapped them all. I'm going into this show cold and unrehearsed; I have no idea how my jokes will land in real time.

Wait, what'd I say about not being nervous? Yeah, strike that. I'm in the middle of the lineup, and with each comic that performs, I feel the nerves creeping up. I was still rewriting my jokes on the subway ride over to Gotham; I feel so underprepared. I run to the bathroom—not to vomit but to practice different takes on each line: Do I deliver it surprised? Angry? Confused? What act-outs do I do? I mime them in the bathroom stall. I haven't had enough time to practice each iteration of my set, to get real-time audience feedback. Shit. *Brosh, why are you doing this to yourself? You volunteered for this torture!* It's not too late to walk away. I can give an excuse—tummy ache, headache—and get out of doing this.

I once read somewhere that artists should do the thing they're most afraid of. *Run* toward *the fear.* Everyone is waiting for me to perform, and I owe it to them to try my best. I steady my shaking hands, my racing heart.

Watching the other comics go up first calms me down. The college student, a math major, shares a cringey story about flunking his first statistics class. The lawyer has a funny bit about a client asking him if he'll also do his taxes *and* dental work. The former firefighter tells a hilarious story about how, after saving people's lives, they'll ask him to go get the stuff they forgot. "Sure. I'll run back into a burning building to grab your cat food and your Costco coupons. *No prob.*"

His sarcasm, delivered in a thick Brooklyn accent, reminds me of Mom's.

Then it's my turn.

"Everybody, please give it up for our next comic, the *very funny* Ambrosia!"

I run up onstage and fist-bump the MC. The house lights are *so* bright, but I try not to let it psych me out.

"My name is Ambrosia Lee," I start, "and I'm a recovering child actor."

Laughs throughout the auditorium. Boom! I'm buoyed. I go in and break the fourth wall.

"God, I sound like an alcoholic at their first AA meeting," I say, and add another tag: "More like Has-Beens Anonymous."

This gets some laughs.

"You may remember me from my seminal work in *Law & Order: SVU*, where I played Dead Asian Girl #3. I got nominated for an Emmy in the category of Best Supporting Female Cadaver . . ." This gets my biggest laugh yet. I wait until the laughter reaches its peak, and *just* as it's on its decrescendo, I finish the thought: ". . . in a Procedural."

My comedic timing is perfect: The crest of laughter from the first half of the joke meets the second crest, and the laughs in the room swell, like waves crashing into each other.

"The competition was *stiff*." Some polite titters.

" 'Over my dead body,' *literally*."

At Dad and Nabi's wedding, I leaned into some corny jokes, and that got laughs. I figure if I tell all the corny corpse puns, the audience will be so exhausted, they'll have no choice but to wave the white flag and laugh. You know how when something's so bad, it becomes good? Like . . . pugs. No disrespect to brachycephalics, but somehow their smushed-up, wrinkly old-man faces are so cute.

"Not to beat a dead horse or anything!"

The sprinkles of laughter are starting to feel like groans. I can feel the energy of the audience shifting. I'm taking this joke too far. I'm dead serious. I've hit a dead end. It's a dead giveaway. I've made a grave mistake. I'm dying up here.

I note this for the future. I have to reel them back. When in doubt, go meta:

"I'm sensing a lot of golf-shirt energy in the crowd? Where are my dads at? Make some noise for these *dad jokes*!"

The sudden, explosive laughter—including from *my* dad, who's slapping his thighs and howling—makes me forget my next line. I take a sip of water from the stool to recover, waiting for the laughter to *die down*. Get it?

Hey, I'm here all night!

"I'm such an overachiever. I was pissed I didn't get Dead Asian Girl #1."

This gets a surprisingly huge laugh. And I realize it's because I'm playing with the model minority stereotype. I make a note to exaggerate my righteous anger when I deliver the line in the future. I think I could milk more laughs. And I need to tighten the wording. Or does that joke just perpetuate stereotypes instead of challenging them?

"But *that* actress already had five years' experience playing dead. Excuse me, I mean, *just being an Asian girl*. Which is basically the same thing. You're just lying there, invisible, while people walk all over you like you don't exist."

I deliver the line super dry. Half the room is dead quiet, tentative, like they don't have permission to laugh, including Annie, who stifles a giggle and looks around like she's afraid she's going to get canceled. But the *other* half of the room explodes—like Mom, Clarissa, and even *Nabi*. She slaps Mom's arm and howls with laughter. And Mom is *letting* her.

And . . . I've officially seen it all.

"It's what every little girl dreams of: getting to be an NPC." There is a huge swell of laughs and cheers—but only in the far corner. Presumably gamers. "Sorry, that means non-player character. Guess you have to be a nerd to get that joke."

The whole room laughs because now *everyone's* in on the joke. Clarissa nudges Annie as they both laugh.

"So my parents are divorced. Give it up for me." People actually cheer. I decide to play with some crowdwork. "Any divorcées in the house?" True to statistics, about 50 percent of the room claps and cheers.

"I think the real reason why they divorced is because of my name: Ambrosia. Mom wanted to name me after a flower, like Heather, Jasmine, or Ivy. Dad wanted stones: Amber, Crystal, Pearl. Their compromise? A fruit salad made of *mayonnaise and marshmallows*." This gets a *huge* laugh, even though it's a little softball corny. Because people think funny names are hilarious. Which is kind of messed up of us as a society if you think about it, but that's a whole other bit.

I researched a ton of ambrosia recipes and felt like *mayonnaise and marshmallows*, with its M-repetition, seemed funnier and sillier than, say, sour cream and pecans, or heavy cream and pineapple, or coconuts and maraschino cherries and mandarin oranges, or any other nonsense that goes into the "salad" that sounds like the culinary brain child of Buddy the Elf—hey, maybe *that* could be added to the bit.

I tag the joke while the laughs are still hot: "Food of the gods, my ass. More like food of the clogged arteries." That gets another swell of chuckles, but not as big as I hoped. Maybe *clogged arteries* doesn't roll off the tongue like . . . *coronary heart disease*? *Atherosclerosis*? Too soon to make a joke about statins? I make a note to rework the line.

"Mom, Dad"—I call out to the audience—"what were you *on* when you named me?"

The crowd cracks up. Mom and Dad exchange a look . . . of solidarity. Does this mean they'll get back together?

This isn't *The Parent Trap*, Brosh; shut it down.

"But my real claim to fame, my pièce de résistance, was when I landed my dream job on a little show called *Jump! Rope! Jungle!*"

Aahs of recognition ripple through the crowd. *Everyone* and their grandmother knows *Jump! Rope! Jungle!* I see lots of nods, and people mouthing *Golly Jee* to each other. Seeing how much the crowd reacts makes me wonder if I should have led my set with the *Jump! Rope!* bit? Maybe I'll try that next time.

"That's right. I was Golly Jee, double-dutcher extraordinaire . . . at least for the first three episodes of season one. I got kicked off the show because I outgrew the part, literally. Hallelujah, puberty."

Crap, for some reason, that joke falls flat. I panic. But Mom makes eye contact with me and nods, giving me the courage to go on.

"The network replaced me with an actor named Jeesun Lee. She was a year younger, three inches shorter, and twenty pounds lighter than me. No one blinked an eye. That was my first important lesson in life. They will always outsource your job to a younger, thinner, cheaper version of you." The room explodes in laughter, salvaging things.

"But what really sucks is to Hollywood, the Other Jees and

I are all the same. We're reduced to a type. A *stereotype.* It can really mess with your head. We're all fighting for the same role, going, 'Pick me! Pick me!' Like . . . like our worth boils down to a single checkbox."

I can feel the energy of the room shifting again. To a more solemn, serious place. It's almost pin-drop quiet. But it's not dead silence because I'm bombing—it's because they're listening. This is precious. I can't squander it. Lara would say, *Don't focus on LPMs. Quality over quantity.* Madame Olga would tell us to lean into the "negative space" of a silence. Pathos in the pain. I finally pick up on what she's been putting down all this time. People want to share in our emotional ups and downs.

I suddenly remember an old street joke in the biz: "The last straw was when I got my royalties in the mail. Sweet, payday!

"It was for . . . two cents. The postage cost more than the check.

"Then when I cashed the check, it *bounced.*

"So now I had to pay a twenty-dollar fee—and I didn't even get to add my two cents."

And that brings down the house.

THE REST OF MY set is a blur. I mess up punch lines I thought I knew cold; I improvise new ones on the spot. The tension between the scripted—the words you've practiced over and over—and the spontaneous—what comes to you on the fly, as you absorb the energy in the room and it absorbs you—is like nothing I have ever experienced before in an audition or on a TV or film set, where there are hundreds of takes until it's perfect and polished and devoid of all feeling. Because this feels raw, and honest, and real.

Teddy was right, in a way: Address the elephant in the room. But it doesn't have to mean making fun of your ugliest physical trait—or anyone else's. The elephant can be emotional, the thing that makes us uncomfortable, or sad, or angry; so let's call it out, head-on. Only hack comics go for the cheap jokes, which divide, insult, or tear people apart.

Humor doesn't have to do that. It can bring people together. It can make people feel at home.

And it took sitting—suffering—through all those toxic mics to realize that.

39

CURTAIN CALL

In the lobby, Mom and Dad are standing side by side. Heads bent toward each other conspiratorially. They're not hurling angry words, like they did the last time they were together. Or the time before that, or all the times before that.

Mom is laughing. Dad, too—he's wiping tears from his eyes.

Wow.

"Ambrosia Lee? Brosh, right?" A woman in her thirties comes up to me. "I don't know if you remember me, but—"

Stan's old assistant. "Sadiya!" I say, surprised.

"Your mom invited me," Sadiya says. Right, Mom mentioned Sadiya was setting out on her own. "You were great tonight! Especially after only, what? A month of doing stand-up?" I nod.

She hands me a card. "Give me a call. Let's set up a time to talk next week."

I just kind of stand there, stunned.

Annie bounds over. "Was that Sadiya Booker?" I nod. "I just

heard she's repping Kym Mendes—she's so hot right now. Brosh, this is huge!" She squeals. "Also, *love* that yellow dress! Slay!"

"Nobody says *slay* anymore, Annie." Clarissa gives Annie a playful bump with her elbow.

"Okayyyy . . ." I look from Annie to Clarissa, who both just dissolve into giggles.

"Brosh, you were *so* good," Clarissa gushes.

"Uh, yeah! She *nailed* it," Annie says. "You're going to blow up one of these days, Brosh."

I wink. "Race ya, Perkins."

"Actually, have you seen Clarissa's stuff?" Annie says. "You guys should write comedy together!"

ME	**CLARISSA**
I don't do improv.	I don't do stand-up.

Clarissa and I look at each other and laugh.

"I mean, I *could* use a new writing buddy," I concede, "since my last one ended up a turd."

"And I *could* use a scene partner," Clarissa says.

"See?" Annie says, pressing her hands together diabolically. "It's *Sister Act*, part deux!"

"Maybe . . . leave the comedy to us?" Clarissa says, and we all laugh again.

"It was so nice to say hi to Cindy—it's been forever," Annie says. "I was fangirling all over her. She is *killing* it with her designs."

"What?"

Annie gives me a pointed look. "I follow your mom online."

I glance over at Mom, who's now . . . cracking jokes with the firefighter?

You don't know what I get up to half the time.

Okay, Mom. You win.

"Your mom said she's going to Korea soon, to meet with some designers. Also something about tying up some loose ends?" Annie shrugs.

Speaking of loose ends—I've spoken with Mom and Dad, and I've decided to start school at LaGuardia in the fall. I read through their curriculum, and there are actually some pretty cool creative writing classes I can take, like a poetry workshop. I think it'll help me with the comedy writing, like with metaphors and stuff. And I can still major in the theater track. I think—okay, I know—a part of me will always want to be in the spotlight.

A guy in a sharp blazer with rolled-up sleeves comes over to us. Clarissa introduces him. "Brosh, this is my friend from Choate, Jung."

I noticed Jung in the audience because (A) he was laughing at all my jokes, and (B) he was cute.

"Wow, Brosh," Jung says. "You were *amazing*."

"Thanks!" We shake hands. And . . . is it corny to say . . . there are *all* the sparks?

Clarissa jabs Jung with her elbow. "Mr. Poetry over here couldn't take his eyes off you."

Jung blushes, big-time.

"You're a poet?" I ask him.

He nods, grinning sheepishly. "This might sound crazy, but I always thought poetry is kind of like stand-up. Especially watching *you* perform."

And . . . there goes my heart.

There's a line of people waiting to talk to me. "Go make your rounds," Annie says, one performer to another.

"Come meet us for dumplings after," Clarissa adds. "We'll text you where."

"I'd like that," I say, staring straight at Jung.

"Me too," he says, smiling back.

Holy dimples.

AT THE FAR CORNER of the room, an older, elegant woman rests on a cane. It's Madame Olga.

"Ambroshka," she says, walking with her usual unhurried grace across the room. The woman knows how to make an entrance.

"Madame Olga!" I breathe out. "What are you doing here? I mean, I didn't expect you— Do you know Lara? Or . . ."

It's kind of awkward, because I'm, like, her least famous student. Madame Olga was a *serious* actor. Back in the day, Madame Olga was the epitome of old Hollywood glamour: young, beautiful, graceful, luminous. Annie told me that she was Orson Welles's muse, or was it Hitchcock's? (Creepy.)

And here I was, making silly jokes onstage.

Madame Olga shakes her head. "Your performance, Ambroshka . . ."

I'm waiting for the laundry list of things I did wrong. I feel like I'm back in her class, pretending to be a squirrel or a lion, or catching butterflies with our breath, or all the other exercises she'd make us do again and again, and I'd never seem to get right.

"I can see how much your training translated to your new medium, Ambroshka," Madame Olga says, in her thick, unplaceable accent. I *think* it's a compliment? "But I urge you to take all the time you need to play. Focus on your craft. You've come a long way, but you have further still to go. We are artists, not factories."

I'm surprised—shocked, really—at the compliment. Madame Olga was so hard to please in class. She never told us what was working, only what needed work.

"Thank you, Madame Olga," I say, really meaning it.

It occurs to me that if Stan were here, that's exactly what he'd do: treat me like a factory. Trot me out on the road with a schlocky marquee—*Child Actor Turned Stand-Up Comic!* He'd take my tight five and water it down to an hour-long special, before I've even honed my craft. My *Jump! Rope!* pedigree might fill the seats in the theater, but it won't keep the audiences coming. And after the inevitable lukewarm-at-best reviews came rolling in, Stan would bail. Again.

It's a long road. Keep at it, Ambrosia Lee.

Madame Olga turns to go. "Wait!" I say. "You don't by any chance—you're not—was that *you* in Tick Tock Diner?"

Madame Olga smiles a *Mona Lisa* smile. Her giant glasses take up most of her face. I can't tell if she heard me. It's impossible to read her expression.

"So much of this business is luck, the vagaries of chance. The only thing you can control is your craft. So be the best you can be, money and fame be damned . . ."

It's almost like Madame Olga's talking to herself.

I FINISH UP THE last of my meet-and-greets. Just as I'm about to head out to meet Clarissa, Annie, and Jung, I see someone darting from the bathroom.

"Teddy?"

"Hey, Brosh, uh . . ." He looks like he got caught naked. "I wasn't sure if I should say hi or not. You looked busy."

"What are *you* doing here?" I demand. I didn't see Teddy at all in the crowd. Was he lurking in the back?

Teddy stares down at his hands. "I know we're not friends . . . or whatever anymore. But you were great up there, Brosh. You were really, *really* funny. And I know you don't need me to tell you that, but . . ." He trails off.

"Thanks, I guess."

"I didn't post my set online," he says. "For whatever it's worth."

"Gee, thanks." My sarcasm is hot and searing. "What about your *likes*?"

("Actually," as Clarissa will tell me later, "that's worth a lot, coming from a content creator.")

"You were right to call me out, Brosh." Teddy stares down at his hands—then catches himself doing it. Stops. "I'm actually going offline for a while. It wasn't good for me."

I kind of can't believe that. I thought Teddy lived for gaining more followers.

Teddy holds out an arm—for a hug? A high five? A fist bump? But he drops it before I can even react.

And then he takes off.

MAYBE SOMEDAY I'LL LOOK back on tonight's performance and think: I was *such* an amateur. This joke needs a quicker setup, that one a stronger punch line, this one needs to be nixed altogether.

But I'm still proud that I got up on that stage and told my story: with honesty and heart. And I'm going to do comedy on *my* terms—slow and steady. And I didn't need to be part of the boys' club to share my truth.

I dropped the mic.

That girl on that stage? She's on her way to something *big*.

Author's Note

I'm obsessed with stand-up comedy.

I follow a bunch of comedians online, and I love how many women comics are out there now, telling their funny stories. Because when I was growing up, stand-up comedy was mostly old dudes telling dirty, offensive jokes. I wondered what it would be like to be a girl navigating this world, trying to make it as a stand-up comedian.

I'd never done comedy before—I'm a watcher, not a doer!—but to research *Ambrosia Lee Drops the Mic*, I studied the form. Suddenly comedy was everywhere: a funny line overheard on the train (people are way too TMI on public transit), the rhythm of a song or poem . . . I kept a comedy journal and jotted down anything and everything, in case I could work it into a bit. I performed almost fifty times over several months, even opening for Jim Gaffigan at Gotham Comedy Club.

Doing stand-up was both exhilarating and excruciating. I'd get on the mic and tell humorous stories (or so I thought!)

about my childhood and family—only to be met with humiliating silence. I was often the only woman and the only person of color in the room, and that made me the target of the other comedians' jokes. I was surprised and saddened by how quickly some young male comics reached for the cheap, insulting punch line, goading each other on. This behavior felt consistent with what I was starting to see in the classrooms and in online discourse. I was a grown woman with a thick skin, and still I felt alienated in the comedy clubs. I worried for all the aspiring, marginalized comedic voices who might get stifled in these spaces.

Humor has an aftertaste. Ambrosia remembers this line in the novel. Early in his career, Gaffigan was told one of his jokes was mean; the accusation made him rethink his comedy and its "aftertaste." I think this line serves as a good reminder of the role of laughter: Are we making jokes at the expense of others? Are we using humor to include—or to exclude? I think about this a lot, and I hope anyone embarking on the road to stand-up bears this in mind, too.

I didn't last long in stand-up comedy—I learned the hard way I should stick to my day job!—but I continue to admire all those comics who are brave enough to go onstage, take their lumps, and get their voices out there. Like Ambrosia Lee.

Hope you enjoyed reading Ambrosia's story and wishing you all the best on your comedy journey!

Acknowledgments

I'd like to thank my family, including my niece and nephews, for their love and support and joy. Thank you to all my friends and family who came out to watch me perform on my "method writing" comedy journey.

I'd like to thank Brett Taylor, to whom this book is dedicated. He patiently listened to every joke I wrote and sat (suffered!) through *So. Many. Open. Mics.* He was there every step of the way. Someone owes this man a sandwich.

To research this novel, I had many helpful conversations with professionals in the performing arts (comedy, theater, TV, film). I'd particularly like to thank Karen Bergreen, Alex Ates, and Alexis Kozak. Thanks also to the Manhattan Comedy School, and Gotham Comedy Club for the stage time.

Huge thanks to my editor, Phoebe Yeh (who also came out to my Gotham show!); Daniela Cortes; and my agent, Sarah Burnes. Thank you to Ellen Oh. Thank you to Barbara Marcus, Judith Haut, Mallory Loehr, Kris Kam, Ray Shappell, and Jamie Johnson; and to the superstars in School and Library: Adrienne Waintraub, Michelle Campbell, Natalie Capogrossi, Jasmine Ferrufino, Katie Halata, and Erica Trotta. Thank you to *all* in the Penguin Random House family for making my stories feel heard.

Lastly, I'd like to thank you, the reader. Without your passion for books (and comedy!), there'd be no this.

Don't miss this laugh-out-loud, provocative read about feeling like a misfit caught between two very different worlds, what it means to belong, and what it takes to build a future for yourself.

Published by Crown Books for Young Readers, an imprint of Random House Children's Books, a division of Penguin Random House LLC, New York.

CHAPTER 1

Origin Story

WHEN YOU HAVE A NAME LIKE ALEJANDRA KIM, teachers always stare at you like you're a typo on the attendance sheet. Each school year, without fail, they look at my face and the roster and back again, like they can't compute my súper-Korean face and my súper-Spanish first name. Multiply that by eight different teachers for eight periods a day, and boom: welcome to my life at Quaker Oats Prep.

I mean, Alejandra is like the "Jessica" of Spanish girl names—basic as all hell. It's not like my parents named me Hermenegilda or Xóchitl. And yet people still find a million and one ways to butcher my name. I've been called:

1. **Alley-JOHN-druh**
   Mr. Landibadeau, our college guidance counselor, who apparently never took Spanish 101. (Hello, the "j" is pronounced like an "h.")

2. **Alexandra**

   Mr. Schwartz, sophomore year, who ironically "Ellis Islanded" me even though he teaches US history.

3. **Ah-leh-CHHHHHAN-durah!**

   Ms. Sanders, junior-year physics. Technically this is correct—the third syllable is pronounced like the "Chan" in "Chanukah." (Hanukah? Hanukkah? You get my point.) But Ms. Sanders was trying *so* hard to sound muy auténtica, which was almost as bad as if she'd just Ellis Islanded my name in the first place. You know, like those annoying people who go to a bodega and order a "CWAH-sson," when the rest of us commoners just say "cruh-SAHNT."

But if you're the one ordering croissants from a corner bodega, that's the least of your pretentious problems.

For the record, I just pronounce it "Ah-lay-HAHN-druh." But I usually tell people to call me "Ally." I say it the easy gringo way: "Alley." As in alley cat, alleyway, back-alley. That's what everyone at Quaker Oats Prep calls me.

Our school's not actually named Quaker Oats. It's officially Anne Austere Preparatory School, named after a Quaker from the 1600s who was literally burned at the stake for trying to better humanity. But everyone just calls us Quaker Oats. We're not like Brearley or Chapin or Dalton. We're more "progressive" (read: "hippie" and "weirdo"). We're like the minor leagues for the big Quaker colleges like Whyder and Swarthmore and Bryn Mawr. Laurel Greenblatt-Watkins, my first and best friend here, says we're a hotbed of granola crunchiness in the middle of Chinatown. I don't know what to think. I'm just a scholarship kid (90 percent). And Ma never lets me forget about that 10 percent we owe each year.

Back in my neighborhood in Queens, they call me "Ale." Except when Ma gets súper pissed, then it's all, "Alejandra Verónica Kim, ¡andate a tu cuarto!"

Papi always used to call me "Aleja-ya."

If I were Dominican or Puerto Rican or Colombian or Mexican, then at least I'd have some solidarity in New York with "mi gente," *my people.* Which might sound vaguely racist, but it is what it is. But my parents are Argentine, and there aren't a whole lot of us here. Both sets of my *parents'* parents were Korean immigrants who were aiming for America-North back in the day but washed up in America-South.

Sidebar: The Korean name for America is Mi-Guk—*Beautiful-Country.* For South America, it's Nam-Mi—*South-of-Beautiful.* Which is all kinds of linguistically fucked up.

It sounds random, how a bunch of Koreans ended up in Argentina. The short answer is immigrant labor exploitation. They were sent over to farm and "populate" Patagonia, but the land was basically a barren desert. The Koreans were like, yeah, nope, and hightailed it to Buenos Aires, where they settled in a villa miseria called Baekgu and sewed clothes all day.

Every time I get upset about something first-world, like how they forgot the ketchup packet with my fries, I have to stop myself and remember: Papi grew up in literal miseryville. He worked in a sweatshop, forced into child labor by his own parents.

That's what happens when you're the kid of immigrants: your whole life is one big guilt trip.

Nothing about my family is "normal." Not even the Spanish we speak, which is all weird and Porteño—aka Buenaryan. Apparently there's a hierarchy within the Latinx community where everyone thinks Argentines are snobby, white European wannabes looking down their noses at the rest of Latin America with their hoity-toity accents and weirder verb conjugations and stubborn refusal to use normal words like "tú"—you. Instead Argentines say "vos," which was súper trending in Spain in the 1500s but has since fallen the way of the pay phone and the postage stamp.

Also, Argentines use the word "che"—hey—a lot, which is how Ernesto Guevara got his nickname.

Anyway, Ma and Papi knew each other as kids back in Baekgu, but they re-met here in New York as adults, and the rest, as they say, is historia.

Che, that was exhausting. What's kind of annoying is how people—adults especially—always expect you to lead with your Origin Story like you're in a Marvel comic, sans the súperpowers. Like, ooh, tell me the exotic story behind your name/face/race/peoples. Walk me through that radioactive spider bite that transformed you into the Súper Freak you are today. (Peter Parker, by the way, is also from Queens.)

I am 94.7 percent sure they wouldn't do that if I looked like my ancestors had stepped off the *Mayflower.*

KNEADING YOUR NEXT READ?

Take a sneak peek at Patricia Park's newest dish on the menu.

NOT YOUR MODEL MINORITY

I'm not one of those TI-84 Plus, Princeton Review, Barron's, Kaplan, Khan, Kumon, hagwon, AP-everything Asian kids with the turtle backpacks crawling all over the 7 train. I used to be. But I'm done with all that.

I just haven't told my parents yet.

Umma went to Bronx Science, like me, and Appa went to Stuyvesant. Unlike me, they were straight A students who went on to Harvard and Yale Law School (Umma), and Carnegie Mellon and Columbia Business School (Appa). That my dad's not a double-Ivy like my mom is kind of a sore spot, and even though he fronts like it isn't, I can tell Appa's still carrying that ginormous chip on his shoulder. But then again, Umma "only" went to Science instead of Stuy—so I guess their "educational disparity" sort of evens out.

These are the things my parents care about. Potato, potahto.

They'd seriously lose it if they found out I was flunking out of Science.

***

OKAY, "FLUNK" IS A STRONG word. Really, I'm just barely passing one class, Global History (70%), and I'm doing "mediocre" (90.1%) in my other classes. My gripe with Global History is that there's got to be more to life than memorizing pointless historical facts about someone else's past, when—shouldn't I be concentrating on my future?

Also, Mr. Doumann keeps confusing me for Jennifer Oh, because to him we're All the Same. Most of my teachers are "woke" or whatever, but Mr. D is a relic from the past—not unlike the very subject he teaches. The DOE should just fire him already, but probably can't (because tenure, teacher's union, pension, etc.). I don't tell Umma and Appa about Mr. Doumann because they'll have no sympathy: *Stop making excuses. Tough it out.* The same things they used to tell my older brother (Oppa to me, Justin to the outside world).

For us Ohs, to be anything less than perfect means you're already a failure. Just ask Oppa.

BACK WHEN I USED TO drink the model minority Kool-Aid, I was all about the Ivy Leagues, too. I thought that was what you were *supposed* to do. The purpose of life was to study hard, get into Harvard/Princeton/Yale, land a corporate job with a sweet 401k, and make babies who would study hard, get into Harvard/Princeton/Yale, etc., and continue your whole miserable corporate life cycle.

My parents are workaholics, which they'd probably take as the compliment it isn't. *Things cost money* is Appa's favorite catchphrase. He works in private equity and has a closetful of suits that I'm constantly picking up and dropping off at the dry cleaners, and I only see his shadow darting into the apartment when he comes home from work, long after I'm already in bed.

Umma's up for managing partner at Leviathan, White & Gross LLP. According to Appa, the promotion is hers to lose. "Your mom's put in the sweat equity, and the other candidate's always blowing off work for"—Appa curls his fingers into sarcastic air quotes—" 'self-care days,'" leaving Umma to pick up the slack. Umma's never been more keyed up and stressed out about this potential promotion. Mostly I try to stay out of her way.

Study hard, get into an Ivy, land a corporate job, make babies. Repeat. These are the Oh Family Core Values.

In other words, it's our American dream.

WHEN I TURNED ONE YEAR old, I grabbed a hundred-dollar bill and my fate was sealed—I'd be financially successful for the rest of my life. Instead of all the other objects (fates) my infant self *could* have reached for during my doljabi ceremony: pencil (scholar), calculator (accountant), paintbrush (artist), golf ball (LPGA pro), iPhone (the next Steve Jobs), and so on.

"Pay up!" Halmoni, ever the hustler, had placed bets with her friends. "My granddaughter's going to be *rich*!"

Apparently she told Haraboji to pay up, too. My grandfather fished for his wallet and grumbled, "알았어." *Fine/Got it/Capisce.* (My Korean's not great, so that's my lost-in-translation translation.)

Haraboji had bet on the bowl of rice—because he wanted me to never go hungry in life.

H&H ARE MY BEDROCK. MY grandparents basically raised me in the kitchen of Melty's, their deli in Midtown. Umma took the bare-minimum maternity leave because it wasn't a good look to take longer than that. She'd drop me off at Melty's each morning on her way to the office. I'd cry and cry, and Halmoni would shush me: "Jackie-ya, you want Umma lose her job? Then how she gonna pay your food? Toys? College? Be good girl, stop crying."

Eventually, I learned to stop crying.

Eventually, I learned to stop depending on my mother at all.

As soon as I was old enough to hold a knife, I was put to work. Which I'm pretty sure is a DOH violation, as well as a Child Services one.

It's the immigrant way.

UMMA, WHOSE IDEA OF "COOKING" is pressing a button to order delivery, insisted on negotiating my pay at Melty's because "I'll not have you repeat my exploited childhood in that kitchen."

But I'd work at Melty's for free. Cooking's my passion. Which I know sounds like some BS you'd write on a college application—*my passions include Ultimate Frisbee, AP Physics, cleaning puppy poop at the animal shelter!*—but I'm actually for real.

I think it's what I want to do for the rest of my life.

BAYSIDE

On Fridays after hagwon—that's Korean for "the school you go to after school because regular school isn't enough"—I head to H&H's house in Bayside for *Burn Off!*

Yes, my Friday-night jam is watching a cooking show with my grandparents and their dog.

Don't judge.

We're sitting at the kitchen table, eating candied kelp. Bingsu, the jindo, sits alert at Haraboji's feet. She's too dignified to lie down and beg for scraps. Her foxlike ears are perked up, like an attack could come from anywhere at any time.

Dogs are funny like that. They are their own people.

Host Dennis appears on the TV screen in his usual toga and laurels. He's so white, he's orange—if that makes any sense—like he's been steeped in Tang. His eyes are the same shade as chlorine pool water. Halmoni is in love with him.

He starts his opening spiel: "Ladies, gentlemen, countrymen!

Lend me your ears! Coming to you *hot* from Kitchen Coliseum, it's *Burn Off!*"

Host Dennis smiles his bleachy grin. When he's not hosting *Burn Off!,* he's flashing his pearls in all those toothpaste ads. Halmoni claps and swoons, and Haraboji and I exchange an eye roll.

The camera pans to a Roman gladiator blowing on a long Viking horn. It's completely culturally inaccurate. I say this as someone flunking Global History.

Speaking of which, my last exam is still crammed in the bottom of my backpack. I don't want to think about it. Just like I don't want to think about how my Global final is next month and I'm so not prepared. I turn my attention back to the screen.

Host Dennis goes, "Today's contestants will slice. They'll dice. They'll fight to the finish! But only one chef will win the crown of—"

The crowd finishes for him: "*Burn Off!* champion!"

The TV fritzes out.

"이놈 . . . !" Haraboji grunts, which is Korean for *You little misbehaving bastard!* He slaps the side of the TV: nothing. It's so old, H&H should have curbed it last millennium. Bingsu snarls at the "misbehaving" TV because she always has Haraboji's back. He's her favorite. Bingsu likes Halmoni okay, and she and I just coexist.

The TV comes back to life.

"—secret ingredients are! Zucchini! Toasted sesame seeds! Red wine vinegar! Prime rib! Strawberry lollipops! And . . .

chocolate-covered ants!" says Host Dennis. "Chefs, you get thirty-seven minutes to complete your dish! So cook off or—"

"Burn Off!" we shout along with the TV audience.

As the TV contestants scurry around the kitchen, my brain is organizing the ingredients, trying to coax them into cohesion. I could see searing off the prime rib with a sesame seed crust, then finishing it in the oven to roast. Sautéed zucchini with a splash of vinegar, like the hobak bokkeum Halmoni made last week. I'd melt down the chocolate-coated ants, forget about the chocolate (because a chocolate mole sauce is too obvious), fish out the ants, and deep-fry them as a frizzled crunchy topping for the meat. But the strawberry lollipops . . .

Halmoni is scribbling the ingredients on the back of an old receipt. "Jackie-ya," she says, "what you think? Most difficult part is chocolate-covered ants."

I laugh. "Seriously, Halmoni? And *not* the lollipops?"

"Easy," she says. "Lollipop instead of kiwi or sugar for beef marinade to make meat tender. Use grater. But chocolate? Make no sense for the dinner."

Then *both* my grandparents give me a look like, *Duh.*

"That's actually pretty brilliant," I say, marveling at how they cracked the riddle of the candy.

I tell them my menu ideas, but Haraboji shakes his head. "No," he says. "Sesame already toasted. Gonna burn and turn bitter, you try to do like that."

Now *I* shake my head. "Haraboji, are you sure? I swear I tried baked sesame from a Middle Eastern bakery—"

"You not believe your own haraboji? Let's go."

He hits pause on the remote and gets up from the table. Never mind that H&H just put in a fourteen-hour day at Melty's. It is *on*.

We round up the *Burn Off!* ingredients or the closest approximations of. We don't have "American" zucchini, but we have hobak—Korean green squash, which is as thick as my forearm. We have the sesame and rice wine vinegar. No prime rib, but sirloin in the freezer. Grape-flavored hard candy. And chocolate-covered . . . chocolate. We make do.

And with that, the three of us are cooking—each of us making our own interpretation of the secret ingredients. I make my sesame beef. Halmoni makes grape-candy-and-soy-marinated galbi, and Haraboji does beef-and-zucchini shish kebabs. We sit down to our smorgasbord, rounded out with leftover pizza from Nino's on Springfield, kimchi, and a jar of kosher dill pickles—which for some reason H&H have an endless supply of.

And it turns out, Haraboji is right. My sesame crust is bitter and burnt.

"Telling you so," Haraboji says, and Halmoni howls at my mistake because there is no mercy in our family.

IT MIGHT SEEM KIND OF random, how we started watching *Burn Off!* But it's the one show the three of us agree on. H&H's English isn't great, so American TV shows are hard for them to follow. My Korean isn't great, so Korean TV is hard for *me* to follow. And H&H are into those Joseon dynasty

K-dramas—the ones where they speak in Ye Olde Korean, which even *Korean* Korean people need subtitles for.

One day we were flipping through the channels, and we landed on this bizarre cooking show. The kitchen set was decorated with marbled columns and ivy. The host, wearing a toga and laurels, announced different challenges: *Make an entrée with six secret ingredients in thirty-seven minutes! A beef dish for less than twenty dollars! A dessert using only a fry pan and a mallet!*

It was a show I didn't have to translate into English and they didn't have to translate into Korean. Food is like the universal language.

Haraboji and I are the true believers—we're in it for the cooking—but Halmoni's favorite part of *Burn Off!* is Host Dennis. Which Haraboji pretends makes him jealous but I think makes him *actually* jealous.

People once ran a cover story on Host Dennis, his husband, their beautiful children, and their McMansion in Malibu. I don't have the heart to tell Halmoni he's off the market.

Haraboji likes Judge Johnny, who brings a down-home, slapsticky element with catchphrases like *You got to eat it to mean it!* and *Prepare to get* burnt*!* My favorite is Judge Stone McMann, who takes a cerebral approach to his food. I own all the cookbooks in his McMann's Authoritative Cookery series. And 55 percent of Burnees are American men ages twenty-one to forty-nine who tune in just for Judge Kelly Sharpe because she's a gorgeous hard-ass who once appeared on the cover of *Maxim* wearing nothing but a bikini-apron thingy.

What can I say? We all got *burnt*.

Umma and Appa have no idea what goes on in my weekends in Bayside.

H&H AND I EAT DINNER and heckle the contestants on TV:

"You forgot the lollipop!"

"Turn on the ice cream maker!"

"Get your steaks off the grill!"

Our running commentary is punctuated by H&H's heckles about my eating and weight:

"Jackie-ya, slow down!" Halmoni tuts. "Too fast eating makes you fat."

"Okay, Halmoni."

"Because Korea, no such thing fat people. Like looking at space alien."

"Okay, Haraboji."

"Because we poor country back then. Now Korea rich, because Samsung and K-pop."

"Okay, Halmoni."

"First time I see fat person, American GI. Haraboji think, '와! 역시 미국이 부자 나라 이구나!'"

Wow! Beautiful-Country (aka America) *sure must be a rich country!*

"Okay, Haraboji."

"GI give us Hershey's chocolate bar." Halmoni smiles, as if remembering that faraway moment. "Best day my life."

"Better than the day you meet me?" Haraboji asks her teasingly.

Halmoni looks me dead in the eyes. "Better."

***

HOST DENNIS MAKES HIS ROUNDS, sticking his mic in each contestant's face and giving them the third degree while the poor chefs are trying to cook. Chef Janice is going Emilia-Romagna style with her dish. Chef Bryce, Normandy. When Host Dennis gets to the last station, it looks like it was hit by a tornado, then a hurricane, then a typhoon: spilled sauces and upside-down pots and pans, false starts every which way.

"Chef Dave," Host Dennis asks, "tell us about your dish!"

The camera zooms in on the ingredients at his workstation: garam masala, Shaoxing wine, rambutan, natto, and kimchi.

Chef Dave doesn't have a clue.

"Absolutely, Dennis—big fan, by the way!" he says. "I'm really embracing the Asian direction of my dish. Because once you go Asian—"

A loud, brassy *GONGGGG!!!* sound effect rings out over the speakers. The studio audience laughs.

I wince. But to my horror, H&H start laughing, too.

"That's *so* offensive!" I say.

"What?" H&H don't get it.

"They're being racist, with that gong," I say.

"Why you take everything so serious?" Haraboji says. "They just having fun."

I say, "Did any of the other chefs go, 'I'm really embracing *European* flavors?' No, they're each cooking a specific region of a specific country! Western Europe's only"—I glance at my phone for the stat—"*three percent* of the world's population.

Meanwhile Chef Dave's got, like, four billion people's food sitting on his counter."

I list the ingredients: Garam masala is from Northern India but is also used in Pakistan, Nepal, Sri Lanka, Bangladesh. Shaoxing wine's from the Zhejiang region of China. Rambutan is native to Malaysia, Thailand, Myanmar, Sri Lanka, Indonesia, Singapore, and the Philippines. Natto's from Japan, and kimchi's Korean, so—why's Chef Dave mixing the colonizer with the colonized?

"Jackie-ya, what you expect?" Halmoni says. "This America. Asian people not famous like Europe people."

"But they can't even get our countries straight," I say. "We're all just 'an Asian direction' to them."

They still don't get it. I hear their obsequious laughter with the customers at Melty's. Customers who are looking down at them *right to their faces.* The bar is so low for them.

But H&H just want to watch the rest of *Burn Off!* in peace. So I let them.

When Chef "Asian direction" Dave gets the win—with a "hot pot" that makes no kind of sense—Haraboji says, "See, Jackie-ya? Now Chef Dave gonna teach American people our food not so scary."

What I hate more than what he says is the *way* he says it. Like we should be most grateful for this Small Win for Asiankind.

I USUALLY SLEEP LIKE A baby at H&H's. Tonight I toss; I turn. The pink flowered blanket, which was probably the same blanket

Umma had when this was her room, is thick and dapdaphae, like I'm being smothered. Outside the window, garbage cans rattle and roll. Queens wildlife. Umma's old posters—Erasure and Depeche Mode, stuff she still rages to when she's having what she calls one of her "han moments"—are giving me the stink eye in the dark from across the room. Oppa's old letters are in a shoebox stowed under the bed since I can't keep them at home.

I can't quiet my mind. I might fail history. Which means I'll sabotage my GPA, which means I won't get into a good college, which means I'll be a failure in life, according to my parents. And I'm only fifteen.

So I do what I always do when I'm stressed or anxious: I start thinking about food.

Recipe-making is my mental happy place. Maybe other people get the same kicks from crosswords or the Rubik's cube. Kind of like how Umma's addicted to sudoku puzzles.

I think about all the other things I could have made with those same *Burn Off!* ingredients.

I make it through four dishes.

Then I drift off to sleep.